Shelve under title

Happy Endings

Other Books by Damon Knight

Novels

A FOR ANYTHING
BEYOND THE BARRIER
HELL'S PAVEMENT

THE OTHER FOOT
THE RITHIAN TERROR

Story Collections

FAR OUT
IN DEEP
OFF CENTER
TURNING ON

THREE NOVELS
WORLD WITHOUT CHILDREN
and THE EARTH QUARTER

Anthologies

BEYOND TOMORROW
A CENTURY OF GREAT SHORT
SCIENCE FICTION NOVELS
A CENTURY OF SCIENCE FICTION
CITIES OF WONDER
THE DARK SIDE
DIMENSION X
FIRST CONTACT
THE GOLDEN ROAD
100 YEARS OF SCIENCE FICTION
THE METAL SMILE
NEBULA AWARD STORIES ONE

NOW BEGINS TOMORROW
ORBIT, VOLUMES 1–14
PERCHANCE TO DREAM
A POCKETFUL OF STARS
A SCIENCE FICTION ARGOSY
SCIENCE FICTION INVENTIONS
THE SHAPE OF THINGS
A SHOCKING THING
TOMORROW AND TOMORROW
TOMORROW $\times$ 4
TOWARD INFINITY
WORLDS TO COME

Translations

ASHES, ASHES
by René Barjavel

13 FRENCH SCIENCE
FICTION STORIES

Biography and Criticism

CHARLES FORT: PROPHET OF
THE UNEXPLAINED

IN SEARCH OF WONDER

Happy Endings

15 STORIES by the
MASTERS OF THE MACABRE

edited by Damon Knight

THE BOBBS-MERRILL COMPANY, INC.

INDIANAPOLIS   NEW YORK

C. 2

M

BL

Acknowledgments

"The Greatest Man in the World" by James Thurber, copyright 1945 by James Thurber, © 1973 by Helen W. Thurber and Rosemary Thurber Sauers. Reprinted from *The Thurber Carnival* by permission of Mrs. James Thurber. Originally published in *The New Yorker*.

"The Way Up to Heaven" by Roald Dahl, copyright © 1959 by Roald Dahl. Reprinted from *Kiss Kiss* by Roald Dahl by permission of Alfred A. Knopf, Inc.

"The Purist" by Ogden Nash, copyright 1935 by The Curtis Publishing Company. Reprinted from *Verses from 1929 On* by Ogden Nash by permission of Little, Brown & Co.

"Father's in the Basement" by Philip José Farmer, copyright © 1972 by Damon Knight. Reprinted from *Orbit 11* by permission of the author and Scott Meredith Literary Agency, Inc.

"Miss Thompson" by W. Somerset Maugham, copyright 1921 by Smart Set Co. Reprinted from *The Trembling of a Leaf* by W. Somerset Maugham by permission of Doubleday & Co., Inc.

"The Damnedest Thing" by Garson Kanin, copyright © 1956 by Esquire, Inc. Reprinted by permission of William Morris Agency, Inc.

"De Mortuis" by John Collier, copyright 1942, © 1969 by John Collier. Reprinted from *Fancies and Goodnights* by John Collier by permission of Harold Matson Co., Inc.

Contents

Introduction

IT IS hard to think of any man or woman whose untimely death would not encourage somebody (a nephew or uncle, say)—lift up his heart, bring a little lightness to his step, a new sparkle to his eye. There are persons whose departures should be celebrated publicly, with fireworks and brass bands, but I am not now speaking of them. I mean those ordinary, unremarkable people who for one reason or another are blots on somebody else's psychic landscape. You and I might not agree or approve, but from a certain viewpoint these persons are unquestionably better off dead. Before we pass judgment, we should examine their histories with care, and it is to allow you this privilege that I have assembled the stories in the present volume.

I hope it will not be thought that in compiling this book I mean to treat murder with excessive levity. "If a man indulges himself in murder," Thomas De Quincey wrote, "very soon he comes to think little of robbing; and from robbing he next comes to drinking and Sabbath-breaking, and from that to incivility and procrastination." With appropriate seriousness, then, let us approach the stories that follow. Many of them are about murder; all are about people whose endings are, in our sense, happy for somebody (you may not always suspect for whom). "Ashes to Ashes," by Nunnally Johnson, to my knowledge has not been reprinted since it appeared in *The Smart Set Anthology,* edited by Burton Rascoe and Groff Conklin, forty years ago. "Father's in the Basement," by Philip José Farmer, was first published in 1972. Between the two, for your delectation and instruction, I have gathered stories by the finest masters of mystery and the macabre. Read them slowly— savor them—and if the faintest suspicion enters your mind that *you* may be one at whose funeral somebody would like to dance, why, so much the better. I leave you with a classic poem (slightly revised for the occasion):

> See the little victim,
> Doesn't give a damn.
> I'm glad I'm not a victim—
> My God! perhaps I am.

DAMON KNIGHT

Madeira Beach
September 18, 1973

Happy Endings

The Greatest Man in the World

✿ BY JAMES THURBER

LOOKING back on it now, from the vantage point of 1950, one can only marvel that it hadn't happened long before it did. The United States of America had been, ever since Kitty Hawk, blindly constructing the elaborate petard by which, sooner or later, it must be hoist. It was inevitable that some day there would come roaring out of the skies a national hero of insufficient intelligence, background, and character successfully to endure the mounting orgies of glory prepared for aviators who stayed up a long time or flew a great distance. Both Lindbergh and Byrd, fortunately for national decorum and international amity, had been gentlemen; so had our other famous aviators. They wore their laurels gracefully, withstood the awful weather of publicity, married excellent women, usually of fine family, and quietly retired to private life and the enjoyment of their varying fortunes. No untoward incidents, on a worldwide scale, marred the perfection of their conduct on the perilous heights of fame. The exception to the rule was, however, bound to occur and it did, in July, 1937, when Jack ("Pal") Smurch, erstwhile mechanic's helper in a small garage in Westfield, Iowa, flew a second-hand, single-motored Bresthaven Dragon-Fly III monoplane all the way around the world, without stopping.

Never before in the history of aviation had such a flight as Smurch's ever been dreamed of. No one had even taken seriously the weird floating auxiliary gas tanks, invention of the mad New Hampshire professor of astronomy, Dr. Charles Lewis Gresham, upon which Smurch placed full reliance. When the garage worker, a slightly built, surly, unprepossessing young man of twenty-two, appeared at Roosevelt Field in early July, 1937, slowly chewing a great quid of scrap tobacco, and announced, "Nobody ain't seen no flyin' yet," the newspapers touched briefly and satirically upon his projected twenty-five-thousand-mile flight. Aeronautical and automotive experts dismissed the idea curtly, implying that it was a hoax, a publicity stunt. The rusty, battered, second-hand plane wouldn't go. The Gresham auxiliary tanks wouldn't work. It was simply a cheap joke.

Smurch, however, after calling on a girl in Brooklyn who worked in the flap-folding department of a large paper-box factory, a girl whom he later described as his "sweet patootie," climbed nonchalantly into his ridiculous plane at dawn of the memorable seventh of July, 1937, spit a curve of tobacco juice into the still air, and took off, carrying with him only a gallon of bootleg gin and six pounds of salami.

When the garage boy thundered out over the ocean the papers were forced to record, in all seriousness, that a mad, unknown young man—his name was variously misspelled —had actually set out upon a preposterous attempt to span the world in a rickety, one-engined contraption, trusting to the long-distance refuelling device of a crazy schoolmaster. When, nine days later, without having stopped once, the tiny plane appeared above San Francisco Bay, headed for New York, spluttering and choking, to be sure, but still magnificently and miraculously aloft, the headlines, which long since had crowded everything else off the front page—even the shooting of the Governor of Illinois by the Vileti gang—swelled to unprecedented size, and the news stories began to run to twenty-five and thirty columns. It was noticeable, however, that the accounts of the epoch-making flight touched rather lightly upon the aviator himself. This was not because facts about the hero as a man were too meager, but because they were too complete.

Reporters, who had been rushed out to Iowa when Smurch's plane was first sighted over the little French coast town of Serly-le-Mer, to dig up the story of the great man's life, had promptly discovered that the story of his life could not be printed. His mother, a sullen short-order cook in a shack restaurant on the edge of a tourists' camping ground near Westfield, met all inquiries as to her son with an angry "Ah, the hell with him; I hope he drowns." His father appeared to be in jail somewhere for stealing spotlights and lap robes from tourists' automobiles; his young brother, a weak-minded lad, had but recently escaped from the Preston, Iowa, Reformatory and was already wanted in several Western towns for the theft of money-order blanks from post offices. These alarming discoveries were still piling up at the very time that Pal Smurch, the greatest hero of the twentieth century, bleareyed, dead for sleep, half-starved, was piloting his crazy junk heap high above the region in which the lamentable story of his private life was being unearthed, headed for New York and a greater glory than any man of his time had ever known.

The necessity for printing some account in the papers of the young man's career and personality had led to a remarkable predicament. It was of course impossible to reveal the facts, for a tremendous popular feeling in favor of the young hero had sprung up, like a grass fire, when he was halfway across Europe on his flight around the globe. He was, therefore, described as a modest chap, taciturn, blond, popular with his friends, popular with girls. The only available snapshot of Smurch, taken at the wheel of a

phony automobile in a cheap photo studio at an amusement park, was touched up so that the little vulgarian
looked quite handsome. His twisted leer was smoothed into
a pleasant smile. The truth was, in this way, kept from the
youth's ecstatic compatriots; they did not dream that the
Smurch family was despised and feared by its neighbors in
the obscure Iowa town, nor that the hero himself, because
of numerous unsavory exploits, had come to be regarded in
Westfield as a nuisance and a menace. He had, the reporters discovered, once knifed the principal of his high school
—not mortally, to be sure, but he had knifed him; and on
another occasion, surprised in the act of stealing an altar-
cloth from a church, he had bashed the sacristan over the
head with a pot of Easter lilies; for each of these offenses he
had served a sentence in the reformatory.

Inwardly, the authorities, both in New York and in
Washington, prayed that an understanding Providence
might, however awful such a thing seemed, bring disaster
to the rusty, battered plane and its illustrious pilot, whose
unheard-of flight had aroused the civilized world to hosan-
nas of hysterical praise. The authorities were convinced
that the character of the renowned aviator was such that
the limelight of adulation was bound to reveal him to all
the world as a congenital hooligan mentally and morally
unequipped to cope with his own prodigious fame. "I
trust," said the Secretary of State, at one of many secret
Cabinet meetings called to consider the national dilemma,
"I trust that his mother's prayer will be answered," by
which he referred to Mrs. Emma Smurch's wish that her
son might be drowned. It was, however, too late for that—
Smurch had leaped the Atlantic and then the Pacific as if
they were millponds. At three minutes after two o'clock on
the afternoon of July 17, 1937, the garage boy brought his
idiotic plane into Roosevelt Field for a perfect three-point
landing.

It had, of course, been out of the question to arrange a
modest little reception for the greatest flier in the history of

the world. He was received at Roosevelt Field with such elaborate and pretentious ceremonies as rocked the world. Fortunately, however, the worn and spent hero promptly swooned, had to be removed bodily from his plane, and was spirited from the field without having opened his mouth once. Thus he did not jeopardize the dignity of this first reception, a reception illumined by the presence of the Secretaries of War and the Navy, Mayor Michael J. Moriarity of New York, the Premier of Canada, Governors Fanniman, Groves, McFeely, and Critchfield, and a brilliant array of European diplomats. Smurch did not, in fact, come to in time to take part in the gigantic hullabaloo arranged at City Hall for the next day. He was rushed to a secluded nursing home and confined to bed. It was nine days before he was able to get up, or to be more exact, before he was permitted to get up. Meanwhile the greatest minds in the country, in solemn assembly, had arranged a secret conference of city, state, and government officials, which Smurch was to attend for the purpose of being instructed in the ethics and behavior of heroism.

On the day that the little mechanic was finally allowed to get up and dress and, for the first time in two weeks, took a great chew of tobacco, he was permitted to receive the newspapermen—this by way of testing him out. Smurch did not wait for questions. "Youse guys," he said—and the *Times* man winced—"youse guys can tell the cockeyed world dat I put it over on Lindbergh, see? Yeh—an' made an ass o' them two frogs." The "two frogs" was a reference to a pair of gallant French fliers who, in attempting a flight only halfway round the world, had, two weeks before, unhappily been lost at sea. The *Times* man was bold enough, at this point, to sketch out for Smurch the accepted formula for interviews in cases of this kind; he explained that there should be no arrogant statements belittling the achievements of other heroes, particularly heroes of foreign nations. "Ah, the hell with that," said Smurch. "I did it, see? I did it, an' I'm talkin' about it." And he did talk about it.

None of this extraordinary interview was, of course, printed. On the contrary, the newspapers, already under the disciplined direction of a secret directorate created for the occasion and composed of statesmen and editors, gave out to a panting and restless world that "Jacky," as he had been arbitrarily nicknamed, would consent to say only that he was very happy and that anyone could have done what he did. "My achievement has been, I fear, slightly exaggerated," the *Times* man's article had him protest, with a modest smile. These newspaper stories were kept from the hero, a restriction which did not serve to abate the rising malevolence of his temper. The situation was, indeed, extremely grave, for Pal Smurch was, as he kept insisting, "rarin' to go." He could not much longer be kept from a nation clamorous to lionize him. It was the most desperate crisis the United States of America had faced since the sinking of the *Lusitania.*

On the afternoon of the twenty-seventh of July, Smurch was spirited away to a conference room in which were gathered mayors, governors, government officials, behaviorist psychologists, and editors. He gave them each a limp, moist paw and a brief unlovely grin. "Hah ya?" he said. When Smurch was seated, the Mayor of New York arose and, with obvious pessimism, attempted to explain what he must say and how he must act when presented to the world, ending his talk with a high tribute to the hero's courage and integrity. The Mayor was followed by Governor Fanniman of New York, who, after a touching declaration of faith, introduced Cameron Spottiswood, Second Secretary of the American Embassy in Paris, the gentleman selected to coach Smurch in the amenities of public ceremonies. Sitting in a chair, with a soiled yellow tie in his hand and his shirt open at the throat, unshaved, smoking a rolled cigarette, Jack Smurch listened with a leer on his lips. "I get ya, I get ya," he cut in, nastily. "Ya want me to ack like a softy, huh? Ya want me to ack like that —— —— baby-faced Lindbergh, huh? Well, nuts to that, see?"

Everyone took in his breath sharply; it was a sigh and a hiss. "Mr. Lindbergh," began a United States Senator, purple with rage, "and Mr. Byrd—" Smurch, who was paring his nails with a jackknife, cut in again. "Byrd!" he exclaimed. "Aw fa God's sake, dat big—" Somebody shut off his blasphemies with a sharp word. A newcomer had entered the room. Everyone stood up, except Smurch, who, still busy with his nails, did not even glance up. "Mr. Smurch," said someone sternly, "the President of the United States!" It had been thought that the presence of the Chief Executive might have a chastening effect upon the young hero, and the former had been, thanks to the remarkable cooperation of the press, secretly brought to the obscure conference room.

A great, painful silence fell. Smurch looked up, waved a hand at the President. "How ya comin'?" he asked, and began rolling a fresh cigarette. The silence deepened. Someone coughed in a strained way. "Geez, it's hot, ain't it?" said Smurch. He loosened two more shirt buttons, revealing a hairy chest and the tattooed word "Sadie" enclosed in a stenciled heart. The great and important men in the room, faced by the most serious crisis in recent American history, exchanged worried frowns. Nobody seemed to know how to proceed. "Come awn, come awn," said Smurch. "Let's get the hell out of here! When do I start cuttin' in on de parties, huh? And what's they goin' to be *in* it?" He rubbed a thumb and forefinger together meaningly. "Money!" exclaimed a state senator, shocked, pale. "Yeh, money," said Pal, flipping his cigarette out of a window. "An' big money." He began rolling a fresh cigarette. "Big money," he repeated, frowning over the rice paper. He tilted back in his chair and leered at each gentleman separately, the leer of an animal that knows its power, the leer of a leopard loose in a bird-and-dog shop. "Aw fa God's sake, let's get some place where it's cooler," he said. "I been cooped up plenty for three weeks!"

Smurch stood up and walked over to an open window,

where he stood staring down into the street, nine floors below. The faint shouting of newsboys floated up to him. He made out his name. "Hot dog!" he cried, grinning, ecstatic. He leaned out over the sill. "You tell 'em, babies!" he shouted down. "Hot diggity-dog!" In the tense little knot of men standing behind him, a quick, mad impulse flared up. An unspoken word of appeal, of command, seemed to ring through the room. Yet it was deadly silent. Charles K. L. Brand, secretary to the Mayor of New York City, happened to be standing nearest Smurch; he looked inquiringly at the President of the United States. The President, pale, grim, nodded shortly. Brand, a tall, powerfully built man, once a tackle at Rutgers, stepped forward, seized the greatest man in the world by his left shoulder and the seat of his pants, and pushed him out the window.

"My God, he's fallen out the window!" cried a quick-witted editor.

"Get me out of here!" cried the President. Several men sprang to his side and he was hurriedly escorted out of a door toward a side entrance of the building. The editor of the Associated Press took charge, being used to such things. Crisply he ordered certain men to leave, others to stay; quickly he outlined a story which all the papers were to agree on, sent two men to the street to handle that end of the tragedy, commanded a senator to sob and two congressmen to go to pieces nervously. In a word, he skillfully set the stage for the gigantic task that was to follow, the task of breaking to a grief-stricken world the sad story of the untimely, accidental death of its most illustrious and spectacular figure.

The funeral was, as you know, the most elaborate, the finest, the solemnest, and the saddest ever held in the United States of America. The monument in Arlington Cemetery, with its clean white shaft of marble and the simple device of a tiny plane carved on its base, is a place for pilgrims, in deep reverence, to visit. The nations of the world paid lofty tributes to little Jacky Smurch, America's greatest hero. At a given hour there were two minutes of silence throughout the nation. Even the inhabitants of the small, bewildered town of Westfield, Iowa, observed this touching ceremony; agents of the Department of Justice saw to that. One of them was especially assigned to stand grimly in the doorway of a little shack restaurant on the edge of the tourists' camping ground just outside the town. There, under his stern scrutiny, Mrs. Emma Smurch bowed her head above two hamburger steaks sizzling on her grill—bowed her head and turned away, so that the Secret Service man could not see the twisted, strangely familiar, leer on her lips.

The Way Up to Heaven

◊ BY ROALD DAHL

ALL her life, Mrs. Foster had had an almost pathological fear of missing a train, a plane, a boat, or even a theater curtain. In other respects, she was not a particularly nervous woman, but the mere thought of being late on occasions like these would throw her into such a state of nerves that she would begin to twitch. It was nothing much—just a tiny vellicating muscle in the corner of the left eye, like a secret wink—but the annoying thing was that it refused to disappear until an hour or so after the train or plane or whatever it was had been safely caught.

It is really extraordinary how in certain people a simple apprehension about a thing like catching a train can grow into a serious obsession. At least half an hour before it was time to leave the house for the station, Mrs. Foster would step out of the elevator all ready to go, with hat and coat and gloves, and then, being quite unable to sit down, she would flutter and fidget about from room to room until her husband, who must have been well aware of her state, finally emerged from his privacy and suggested in a cool dry voice that perhaps they had better get going now, had they not?

Mr. Foster may possibly have had a right to be irritated by this foolishness of his wife's, but he could have had no excuse for increasing her misery by keeping her waiting unnecessarily. Mind you, it is by no means certain that this is what he did, yet whenever they were to go somewhere, his timing was so accurate—just a minute or two late, you understand—and his manner so bland that it was hard to believe he wasn't purposely inflicting a nasty private little torture of his own on the unhappy lady. And one thing he must have known—that she would never dare to call out and tell him to hurry. He had disciplined her too well for that. He must also have known that if he was prepared to wait even beyond the last moment of safety, he could drive her nearly into hysterics. On one or two special occasions in the later years of their married life, it seemed almost as though he had *wanted* to miss the train simply in order to intensify the poor woman's suffering.

Assuming (though one cannot be sure) that the husband was guilty, what made his attitude doubly unreasonable was the fact that, with the exception of this one small irrepressible foible, Mrs. Foster was and always had been a good and loving wife. For over thirty years, she had served him loyally and well. There was no doubt about this. Even she, a very modest woman, was aware of it, and although she had for years refused to let herself believe that Mr. Foster would ever consciously torment her, there had been times recently when she had caught herself beginning to wonder.

Mr. Eugene Foster, who was nearly seventy years old, lived with his wife in a large six-story house on East Sixty-second Street, and they had four servants. It was a gloomy place, and few people came to visit them. But on this particular morning in January, the house had come alive and there was a great deal of bustling about. One maid was distributing bundles of dust sheets to every room, while another was draping them over the furniture. The butler was bringing down suitcases and putting them in the hall.

The cook kept popping up from the kitchen to have a word with the butler, and Mrs. Foster herself, in an old-fashioned fur coat and with a black hat on the top of her head, was flying from room to room and pretending to supervise these operations. Actually, she was thinking of nothing at all except that she was going to miss her plane if her husband didn't come out of his study soon and get ready.

"What time is it, Walker?" she said to the butler as she passed him.

"It's ten minutes past nine, madam."

"And has the car come?"

"Yes, madam, it's waiting. I'm just going to put the luggage in now."

"It takes an hour to get to Idlewild," she said. "My plane leaves at eleven. I have to be there half an hour beforehand for the formalities. I shall be late. I just *know* I'm going to be late."

"I think you have plenty of time, madam," the butler said kindly. "I warned Mr. Foster that you must leave at nine-fifteen. There's still another five minutes."

"Yes, Walker, I know, I know. But get the luggage in quickly, will you please?"

She began walking up and down the hall, and whenever the butler came by, she asked him the time. This, she kept telling herself, was the *one* plane she must not miss. It had taken months to persuade her husband to allow her to go. If she missed it, he might easily decide that she should cancel the whole thing. And the trouble was that he insisted on coming to the airport to see her off.

"Dear God," she said aloud, "I'm going to miss it. I know, I know, I *know* I'm going to miss it." The little muscle beside the left eye was twitching madly now. The eyes themselves were very close to tears.

"What time is it, Walker?"

"It's eighteen minutes past, madam."

"Now I really *will* miss it!" she cried. "Oh, I wish he would come!"

This was an important journey for Mrs. Foster. She was going all alone to Paris to visit her daughter, her only child, who was married to a Frenchman. Mrs. Foster didn't care much for the Frenchman, but she was fond of her daughter, and, more than that, she had developed a great yearning to set eyes on her three grandchildren. She knew them only from the many photographs that she had received and that she kept putting up all over the house. They were beautiful, these children. She doted on them, and each time a new picture arrived, she would carry it away and sit with it for a long time, staring at it lovingly and searching the small faces for signs of that old satisfying blood likeness that meant so much. And now, lately, she had come more and more to feel that she did not really wish to live out her days in a place where she could not be near these children, and have them visit her, and take them for walks, and buy them presents, and watch them grow. She knew, of course, that it was wrong and in a way disloyal to have thoughts like these while her husband was still alive. She knew also that although he was no longer active in his many enterprises, he would never consent to leave New York and live in Paris. It was a miracle that he had ever agreed to let her fly over there alone for six weeks to visit them. But, oh, how she wished she could live there always, and be close to them!

"Walker, what time is it?"

"Twenty-two minutes past, madam."

As he spoke, a door opened and Mr. Foster came into the hall. He stood for a moment, looking intently at his wife, and she looked back at him—at this diminutive but still quite dapper old man with the huge bearded face that bore such an astonishing resemblance to those old photographs of Andrew Carnegie.

"Well," he said, "I suppose perhaps we'd better get going fairly soon if you want to catch that plane."

"*Yes*, dear—*yes!* Everything's ready. The car's waiting."

"That's good," he said. With his head over to one side, he

was watching her closely. He had a peculiar way of cocking the head and then moving it in a series of small, rapid jerks. Because of this and because he was clasping his hands up high in front of him, near the chest, he was somehow like a squirrel standing there—a quick clever old squirrel from the park.

"Here's Walker with your coat, dear. Put it on."

"I'll be with you in a moment," he said. "I'm just going to wash my hands."

She waited for him, and the tall butler stood beside her, holding the coat and the hat.

"Walker, will I miss it?"

"No, madam," the butler said. "I think you'll make it all right."

Then Mr. Foster appeared again, and the butler helped him on with his coat. Mrs. Foster hurried outside and got into the hired Cadillac. Her husband came after her, but he walked down the steps of the house slowly, pausing halfway to observe the sky and to sniff the cold morning air.

"It looks a bit foggy," he said as he sat down beside her in the car. "And it's always worse out there at the airport. I shouldn't be surprised if the flight's cancelled already."

"Don't say that, dear—*please.*"

They didn't speak again until the car had crossed over the river to Long Island.

"I arranged everything with the servants," Mr. Foster said. "They're all going off today. I gave them half pay for six weeks and told Walker I'd send him a telegram when we wanted them back."

"Yes," she said. "He told me."

"I'll move into the club tonight. It'll be a nice change staying at the club."

"Yes, dear. I'll write to you."

"I'll call in at the house occasionally to see that everything's all right and to pick up the mail."

"But don't you really think Walker should stay there all the time to look after things?" she asked meekly.

"Nonsense. It's quite unnecessary. And anyway, I'd have to pay him full wages."

"Oh, yes," she said. "Of course."

"What's more, you never know what people get up to when they're left alone in a house," Mr. Foster announced, and with that he took out a cigar and, after snipping off the end with a silver cutter, lit it with a gold lighter.

She sat still in the car with her hands clasped together tight under the rug.

"Will you write to me?" she asked.

"I'll see," he said. "But I doubt it. You know I don't hold with letter-writing unless there's something specific to say."

"Yes, dear, I know. So don't you bother."

They drove on, along Queens Boulevard, and as they approached the flat marshland on which Idlewild was built, the fog began to thicken and the car had to slow down.

"Oh, dear!" cried Mrs. Foster. "I'm *sure* I'm going to miss it now! What time is it?"

"Stop fussing," the old man said. "It doesn't matter anyway. It's bound to be cancelled now. They never fly in this sort of weather. I don't know why you bothered to come out."

She couldn't be sure, but it seemed to her that there was suddenly a new note in his voice, and she turned to look at him. It was difficult to observe any change in his expression under all that hair. The mouth was what counted. She wished, as she had so often before, that she could see the mouth clearly. The eyes never showed anything except when he was in a rage.

"Of course," he went on, "if by any chance it *does* go, then I agree with you—you'll be certain to miss it now. Why don't you resign yourself to that?"

She turned away and peered through the window at the fog. It seemed to be getting thicker as they went along, and now she could only just make out the edge of the road and the margin of grassland beyond it. She knew that her husband was still looking at her. She glanced back at him again, and this time she noticed with a kind of horror that he was staring intently at the little place in the corner of her left eye where she could feel the muscle twitching.

"Won't you?" he said.

"Won't I what?"

"Be sure to miss it now if it goes. We can't drive fast in this muck."

He didn't speak to her any more after that. The car crawled on and on. The driver had a yellow lamp directed onto the edge of the road, and this helped him to keep going. Other lights, some white and some yellow, kept coming out of the fog toward them, and there was an especially bright one that followed close behind them all the time.

Suddenly, the driver stopped the car.

"There!" Mr. Foster cried. "We're stuck. I knew it."

"No, sir," the driver said, turning round. "We made it. This is the airport."

Without a word, Mrs. Foster jumped out and hurried through the main entrance into the building. There was a mass of people inside, mostly disconsolate passengers standing around the ticket counters. She pushed her way through and spoke to the clerk.

"Yes," he said. "Your flight is temporarily postponed. But please don't go away. We're expecting this weather to clear any moment."

She went back to her husband who was still sitting in the car and told him the news. "But don't you wait, dear," she said. "There's no sense in that."

"I won't," he answered. "So long as the driver can get me back. Can you get me back, driver?"

"I think so," the man said.

"Is the luggage out?"

"Yes, sir."

"Good-bye, dear," Mrs. Foster said, leaning into the car and giving her husband a small kiss on the coarse grey fur of his cheek.

"Good-bye," he answered. "Have a good trip."

The car drove off, and Mrs. Foster was left alone.

The rest of the day was a sort of nightmare for her. She sat for hour after hour on a bench, as close to the airline counter as possible, and every thirty minutes or so she would get up and ask the clerk if the situation had changed. She always received the same reply—that she must continue to wait, because the fog might blow away at any moment. It wasn't until after six in the evening that the loudspeakers finally announced that the flight had been postponed until eleven o'clock the next morning.

Mrs. Foster didn't quite know what to do when she heard this news. She stayed sitting on her bench for at least another half-hour, wondering, in a tired, hazy sort of way, where she might go to spend the night. She hated to leave the airport. She didn't wish to see her husband. She was terrified that in one way or another he would eventually manage to prevent her from getting to France. She would have liked to remain just where she was, sitting on the bench the whole night through. That would be the safest. But she was already exhausted, and it didn't take her long to realize that this was a ridiculous thing for an elderly lady to do. So in the end she went to a phone and called the house.

Her husband, who was on the point of leaving for the club, answered it himself. She told him the news, and asked whether the servants were still there.

"They've all gone," he said.

"In that case, dear, I'll just get myself a room somewhere for the night. And don't you bother yourself about it at all."

"That would be foolish," he said. "You've got a large house here at your disposal. Use it."

"But, dear, it's *empty.*"

"Then I'll stay with you myself."

"There's no food in the house. There's nothing."

"Then eat before you come in. Don't be so stupid, woman. Everything you do, you seem to want to make a fuss about it."

"Yes," she said. "I'm sorry. I'll get myself a sandwich here, and then I'll come on in."

Outside, the fog had cleared a little, but it was still a long, slow drive in the taxi, and she didn't arrive back at the house on Sixty-second Street until fairly late.

Her husband emerged from his study when he heard her coming in. "Well," he said, standing by the study door, "how was Paris?"

"We leave at eleven in the morning," she answered. "It's definite."

"You mean if the fog clears."

"It's clearing now. There's a wind coming up."

"You look tired," he said. "You must have had an anxious day."

"It wasn't very comfortable. I think I'll go straight to bed."

"I've ordered a car for the morning," he said. "Nine o'clock."

"Oh, thank you, dear. And I certainly hope you're not going to bother to come all the way out again to see me off."

"No," he said slowly. "I don't think I will. But there's no reason why you shouldn't drop me at the club on your way."

She looked at him, and at that moment he seemed to be standing a long way off from her, beyond some borderline. He was suddenly so small and far away that she couldn't be sure what he was doing, or what he was thinking, or even what he was.

"The club is downtown," she said. "It isn't on the way to the airport."

"But you'll have plenty of time, my dear. Don't you want to drop me at the club?"

"Oh, yes—of course."

"That's good. Then I'll see you in the morning at nine."

She went up to her bedroom on the third floor, and she was so exhausted from her day that she fell asleep soon after she lay down.

Next morning, Mrs. Foster was up early, and by eight-thirty she was downstairs and ready to leave.

Shortly after nine, her husband appeared. "Did you make any coffee?" he asked.

"No, dear. I thought you'd get a nice breakfast at the club. The car is here. It's been waiting. I'm all ready to go."

They were standing in the hall—they always seemed to be meeting in the hall nowadays—she with her hat and coat and purse, he in a curiously cut Edwardian jacket with high lapels.

"Your luggage?"

"It's at the airport."

"Ah, yes," he said. "Of course. And if you're going to take me to the club first, I suppose we'd better get going fairly soon, hadn't we?"

"Yes!" she cried. "Oh, yes—*please!*"

"I'm just going to get a few cigars. I'll be right with you. You get in the car."

She turned and went out to where the chauffeur was standing, and he opened the car door for her as she approached.

"What time is it?" she asked him.

"About nine-fifteen."

Mr. Foster came out five minutes later, and watching him as he walked slowly down the steps, she noticed that his legs were like goat's legs in those narrow stovepipe trousers that he wore. As on the day before, he paused halfway down to sniff the air and to examine the sky. The weather was still not quite clear, but there was a wisp of sun coming through the mist.

"Perhaps you'll be lucky this time," he said as he settled himself beside her in the car.

"Hurry, please," she said to the chauffeur. "Don't bother about the rug. I'll arrange the rug. Please get going. I'm late."

The man went back to his seat behind the wheel and started the engine.

"*Just* a moment!" Mr. Foster said suddenly. "Hold it a moment, chauffeur, will you?"

"What is it, dear?" She saw him searching the pockets of his overcoat.

"I had a little present I wanted you to take to Ellen," he said. "Now, where on earth is it? I'm sure I had it in my hand as I came down."

"I never saw you carrying anything. What sort of present?"

"A little box wrapped up in white paper. I forgot to give it to you yesterday. I don't want to forget it today."

"A little box!" Mrs. Foster cried. "I never saw any little box!" She began hunting frantically in the back of the car.

Her husband continued searching through the pockets of his coat. Then he unbuttoned the coat and felt around in his jacket. "Confound it," he said, "I must've left it in my bedroom. I won't be a moment."

"Oh, *please!*" she cried. "We haven't got time! *Please* leave it! You can mail it. It's only one of those silly combs anyway. You're always giving her combs."

"And what's wrong with combs, may I ask?" he said, furious that she should have forgotten herself for once.

"Nothing, dear, I'm sure. But . . ."

"Stay here!" he commanded. "I'm going to get it."

"Be quick, dear! Oh, *please* be quick!"

She sat still, waiting and waiting.

"Chauffeur, what time is it?"

The man had a wristwatch, which he consulted. "I make it nearly nine-thirty."

"Can we get to the airport in an hour?"

"Just about."

At this point, Mrs. Foster suddenly spotted a corner of something white wedged down in the crack of the seat on the side where her husband had been sitting. She reached over and pulled out a small paper-wrapped box, and at the same time she couldn't help noticing that it was wedged down firm and deep, as though with the help of a pushing hand.

"Here it is!" she cried. "I've found it! Oh, dear, and now

he'll be up there forever searching for it! Chauffeur, quickly—run in and call him down, will you please?"

The chauffeur, a man with a small rebellious Irish mouth, didn't care very much for any of this, but he climbed out of the car and went up the steps to the front door of the house. Then he turned and came back. "Door's locked," he announced. "You got a key?"

"Yes—wait a minute." She began hunting madly in her purse. The little face was screwed up tight with anxiety, the lips pushed outward like a spout.

"Here it is! No—I'll go myself. It'll be quicker. I know where he'll be."

She hurried out of the car and up the steps to the front door, holding the key in one hand. She slid the key into the keyhole and was about to turn it—and then she stopped. Her head came up, and she stood there absolutely motionless, her whole body arrested right in the middle of all this hurry to turn the key and get into the house, and she waited —five, six, seven, eight, nine, ten seconds, she waited. The way she was standing there, with her head in the air and the body so tense, it seemed as though she were listening for the repetition of some sound that she had heard a moment before from a place far away inside the house.

Yes—quite obviously she was listening. Her whole attitude was a *listening* one. She appeared actually to be moving one of her ears closer and closer to the door. Now it was right up against the door, and for still another few seconds she remained in that position, head up, ear to door, hand on key, about to enter but not entering, trying instead, or so it seemed, to hear and to analyze these sounds that were coming faintly from this place deep within the house.

Then, all at once, she sprang to life again. She withdrew the key from the door and came running back down the steps.

"It's too late!" she cried to the chauffeur. "I can't wait for him, I simply can't. I'll miss the plane. Hurry now, driver, hurry! To the airport!"

The chauffeur, had he been watching her closely, might
have noticed that her face had turned absolutely white and
that the whole expression had suddenly altered. There was
no longer that rather soft and silly look. A peculiar hard-
ness had settled itself upon the features. The little mouth,
usually so flabby, was now tight and thin, the eyes were
bright, and the voice, when she spoke, carried a new note
of authority.

"Hurry, driver, hurry!"

"Isn't your husband traveling with you?" the man asked,
astonished.

"Certainly not! I was only going to drop him at the club.
It won't matter. He'll understand. He'll get a cab. Don't sit
there talking, man. *Get going!* I've got a plane to catch for
Paris!"

With Mrs. Foster urging him from the back seat, the man
drove fast all the way, and she caught her plane with a few
minutes to spare. Soon she was high up over the Atlantic,
reclining comfortably in her airplane chair, listening to
the hum of the motors, heading for Paris at last. The new
mood was still with her. She felt remarkably strong and, in
a queer sort of way, wonderful. She was a trifle breathless
with it all, but this was more from pure astonishment at
what she had done than anything else, and as the plane
flew farther and farther away from New York and East
Sixty-second Street, a great sense of calmness began to
settle upon her. By the time she reached Paris, she was just
as strong and cool and calm as she could wish.

She met her grandchildren, and they were even more
beautiful in the flesh than in their photographs. They were
like angels, she told herself, so beautiful they were. And
every day she took them for walks, and fed them cakes, and
bought them presents, and told them charming stories.

Once a week, on Tuesdays, she wrote a letter to her husband—a nice, chatty letter—full of news and gossip, which
always ended with the words "Now be sure to take your
meals regularly, dear, although this is something I'm

afraid you may not be doing when I'm not with you."

When the six weeks were up, everybody was sad that she had to return to America, to her husband. Everybody, that is, except her. Surprisingly, she didn't seem to mind as much as one might have expected, and when she kissed them all good-bye, there was something in her manner and in the things she said that appeared to hint at the possibility of a return in the not too distant future.

However, like the faithful wife she was, she did not overstay her time. Exactly six weeks after she had arrived, she sent a cable to her husband and caught the plane back to New York.

Arriving at Idlewild, Mrs. Foster was interested to observe that there was no car to meet her. It is possible that she might even have been a little amused. But she was extremely calm and did not overtip the porter who helped her into a taxi with her baggage.

New York was colder than Paris, and there were lumps of dirty snow lying in the gutters of the streets. The taxi drew up before the house on Sixty-second Street, and Mrs. Foster persuaded the driver to carry her two large cases to the top of the steps. Then she paid him off and rang the bell. She waited, but there was no answer. Just to make sure, she rang again, and she could hear it tinkling shrilly far away in the pantry, at the back of the house. But still no one came.

So she took out her own key and opened the door herself.

The first thing she saw as she entered was a great pile of mail lying on the floor where it had fallen after being slipped through the letter hole. The place was dark and cold. A dust sheet was still draped over the grandfather clock. In spite of the cold, the atmosphere was peculiarly oppressive, and there was a faint but curious odor in the air that she had never smelled before.

She walked quickly across the hall and disappeared for a moment around the corner to the left, at the back. There was something deliberate and purposeful about this action; she had the air of a woman who is off to investigate a rumor or to confirm a suspicion. And when she returned a few seconds later, there was a little glimmer of satisfaction on her face.

She paused in the center of the hall, as though wondering what to do next. Then, suddenly, she turned and went across into her husband's study. On the desk she found his address book, and after hunting through it for a while she picked up the phone and dialed a number.

"Hello," she said. "Listen—this is Nine East Sixty-second Street. . . . Yes, that's right. Could you send someone round as soon as possible, do you think? Yes, it seems to be stuck between the second and third floors. At least, that's where the indicator's pointing. . . . Right away? Oh, that's very kind of you. You see, my legs aren't any too good for walking up a lot of stairs. Thank you so much. Good-bye."

She replaced the receiver and sat there at her husband's desk, patiently waiting for the man who would be coming soon to repair the elevator.

The Purist

BY OGDEN NASH

I GIVE you now Professor Twist,
A conscientious scientist.
Trustees exclaimed, "He never bungles!"
And sent him off to distant jungles.
Camped on a tropic riverside,
One day he missed his loving bride.
She had, the guide informed him later,
Been eaten by an alligator.
Professor Twist could not but smile.
"You mean," he said, "a crocodile."

Father's in the Basement

BY PHILIP JOSÉ FARMER

THE TYPEWRITER had clattered for three and a half days. It must have stopped now and then, but never when Millie was awake. She had fallen asleep perhaps five times during that period, though something always aroused her after fifteen minutes or so of troubled dreams.

Perhaps it was the silence that hooked her and drew her up out of the thick waters. As soon as she became fully conscious, however, she heard the clicking of the typewriter start up.

The upper part of the house was almost always clean and neat. Millie was only eleven, but she was the only female in the household, her mother having died when Millie was nine. Millie never cleaned the basement because her father forbade it.

The big basement room was his province. There he kept all his reference books, and there he wrote at a long desk. This room and the adjoining furnace-utility room constituted her father's country (he even did the washing), and if it was a mess to others, it was order to him. He could reach into the chaos and pluck out anything he wanted with no hesitation.

Her father was a free-lance writer, a maker of literary soups, a potboiler cook. He wrote short stories and articles for men's and women's magazines under male or female names, science fiction novels, trade magazine articles, and an occasional Gothic. Sometimes he got a commission to write a novel based on a screenplay.

"I'm the poor man's Frederick Faust," her father had said many times. "I won't be remembered ten years from now. Not by anyone who counts. I want to be remembered, baby, to be reprinted through the years as a classic, to be written of, talked of, as a great writer. And so . . ."

And so, on the left side of his desk, in a file basket, was half a manuscript, three hundred pages. Pop had been working on it, on and off, mostly off, for fifteen years. It was to be his masterpiece, the one book that would transcend all his hackwork, the book that would make the public cry "Wow!"; the one book by him that would establish him as a Master. ("Capital M, baby!") It would put his name in the *Encyclopaedia Britannica;* he would not take up much space in it; a paragraph was all he asked.

He had patted her hand and said, "And so when you tell people your name, they'll say, 'You aren't the daughter of the great Brady X. Donaldson? You are? Fantastic! And what was he really like, your father?'"

And then, reaching out and stroking her pointed chin, he had said, "I hope you can be proud of having a father who wrote at least one great book, baby. But, of course, you'll be famous in your own right. You have unique abilities, and don't you ever forget it. A kid with your talents has to grow up into a famous person. I only wish that I could be around. . . ."

He did not go on. Neither of them cared to talk about his heart "infraction," as he insisted on calling it.

She had not commented on his remark about her "abilities." He was not aware of their true breadth and depth, nor did she want him to be aware.

The phone rang. Millie got up out of the chair and

walked back and forth in the living room. The typewriter had not even hesitated when the phone rang. Her father was stopping for nothing, and he might not even have heard the phone, so intent was he. This was the only chance he would ever get to finish his Work ("Capital W, baby!"), and he would sit at his desk until it was done. Yet she knew that he could go on like this only so long before falling apart.

She knew who was calling. It was Mrs. Coombs, the secretary of Mr. Appleton, the principal of Dashwood Grade School. Mrs. Coombs had called every day. The first day, Millie had told Mrs. Coombs that she was sick. No, her father could not come to the phone because he had a very deadly schedule to meet. Millie had opened the door to the basement and turned the receiver of the phone so that Mrs. Coombs could hear the heavy and unceasing typing.

Millie spoke through her nose and gave a little cough now and then, but Mrs. Coombs's voice betrayed disbelief.

"My father knows I have this cold, and so he doesn't see why he should be bothered telling anybody that I have it. He knows I have it. No, it's not bad enough to go to the doctor for it. No, my father will not come to the phone now. You wouldn't like it if he had to come to the phone now. You can be sure of that.

"No, I can't promise you he'll call before five, Mrs. Coombs. He doesn't want to stop while he's going good, and I doubt very much he'll be stopping at five. Or for some time after, if I know my father. In fact, Mrs. Coombs, I can't promise anything except that he won't stop until he's ready to stop."

Mrs. Coombs had made some important-sounding noises, but she finally said she'd call back tomorrow. That is, she would unless Millie was at school in the morning, with a note from her father, or unless her father called in to say that she was still sick.

The second day, Mrs. Coombs had phoned again, and Millie had let the ringing go on until she could stand it no longer.

"I'm sorry, Mrs. Coombs, but I feel lots worse. And my father didn't call in, and won't, because he is still typing. Here, I'll hold the phone to the door so you can hear him."

Millie waited until Mrs. Coombs seemed to have run down.

"Yes, I can appreciate your position, Mrs. Coombs, but he won't come, and I won't ask him to. He has so little time left, you know, and he has to finish this one book, and he isn't listening to any such thing as common sense or . . . No, Mrs. Coombs, I'm not trying to play on your sympathies with this talk about his heart trouble.

"Father is going to sit there until he's done. He said this is his lifework, his only chance for immortality. He doesn't believe in life after death, you know. He says that a man's only chance for immortality is in the deeds he does or the works of art he produces.

"Yes, I know it's a peculiar situation, and he's a peculiar man, and I should be at school."

And you, Mrs. Coombs, she thought, you think I'm a very peculiar little girl, and you don't really care that I'm not at school today. In fact, you like it that I'm not there because you get the chills every time you see me.

"Yes, Mrs. Coombs, I know you'll have to take some action, and I don't blame you for it. You'll send somebody out to check; you have to do it because the rules say you have to, not because you think I'm lying.

"But you can hear my father typing, can't you? You surely don't think that's a recording of a typist, do you?"

She shouldn't have said that, because now Mrs. Coombs would be thinking exactly that.

She went into the kitchen and made more coffee. Pop had forbidden her coffee until she was fourteen, but she needed it to keep going. Besides, he wouldn't know anything about it. He had told her, just before he had felt the first pain, that he could finish the Work in eighty-four to ninety-six hours if he were uninterrupted and did not have to stop because of exhaustion or another attack.

"I've got it all composed up here," he had said, pointing

a finger at his temple. "It's just a matter of sitting down and staying down, and that's what I'm going to do, come hell or high water, come infraction or infarction. In ten minutes, I'm going down into my burrow, and I'm not coming back up until I'm finished."

"But, Pop," Millie had said, "I don't see how you can. Exercise or excitement is what brings on an attack. . . ."

"I got my pills, and I'll rest if I have to and take longer," he had said. "So it takes two weeks? But I don't think it will. Listen, Millie," and he had taken her hand in his and looked into her eyes as if they were binoculars pointing into a fourth dimension, "I'm depending on you more than on my pills or even on myself. You'll not let anybody or anything interfere, will you? I know I shouldn't ask you to stay home from school, but this is more important than school. I really need you. I can't afford to put this off any longer. I don't have the time. You know that."

He had released her hand and started toward the basement door, saying, "This is it; here goes," when his face had twisted and he had grabbed his chest.

But that had not stopped him.

The phone rang. It was, she knew, Mrs. Coombs again.

Mrs. Coombs's voice was as thin as river ice in late March.

"You tell your father that officers will be on their way to your house within a few minutes. They'll have a warrant to enter."

"You're causing a lot of trouble and for no good reason," Millie said. "Just because you don't like me . . ."

"Well, I never!" Mrs. Coombs said. "You know very well that I'm doing what I have to and, in fact, I've been overly lenient in this case. There's no reason in the world why your father can't come to the phone. . . ."

"I told you he had to finish his novel," Millie said. "That's all the reason he needs."

She hung up the phone and then stood by the door for a moment, listening to the typing below. She turned and looked through the kitchen door at the clock on the wall. It was almost twelve. She doubted that anybody would come during the lunch hour, despite what Mrs. Coombs said. That gave her—her father, rather—another hour. And then she would see what she could do.

She tried to eat but could get down only half the liverwurst and lettuce sandwich. She wrapped the other half and put it back into the refrigerator. She looked at herself in the small mirror near the wall clock. She, who could not afford to lose an ounce, had shed pounds during the past three and a half days. As if they were on scales, her cheekbones had risen while her eyes had sunk. The dark brown irises and the bloodshot whites of her eyes looked like two fried eggs with ketchup that someone had thrown against a wall.

She smiled slightly at the thought, but it hurt her to see her face. She looked like a witch and always would.

"But you're only eleven!" her father had boomed at her. "Is it a tragedy at eleven because the boys haven't asked you for a date yet? My God, when I was eleven, we didn't ask girls for dates. We hated girls!"

Yet his Great Work started with the first-love agonies of a boy of eleven, and he had admitted long ago that the boy was himself.

Millie sighed again and left the mirror. She cleaned the front room but did not use the vacuum cleaner because she wanted to hear the typewriter keys. The hour passed, and the doorbell rang.

She sat down in a chair. The doorbell rang again and again. Then there was silence for a minute, followed by a fist pounding on the door.

Millie got up from the chair but went to the door at the top of the basement steps and opened it. She breathed deeply, made a face, went down the wooden steps and around the corner at the bottom and looked down the long room with its white-painted cement blocks and pine paneling. She could not see her father because a tall and broad dark mahogany bookcase in the middle of the room formed the back of what he called his office. The chair and desk were on the other side, but she could see the file basket on the edge of the desk. Her practiced eye told her that the basket held almost five hundred pages, not counting the carbon copies.

The typewriter clattered away. After a while, she went back up the steps and across to the front door. She opened the peephole and looked through. Two of the three looked as if they could be plainclothesmen. The third was the tall, beefy, red-faced truant officer.

"Hello, Mr. Tavistock," she said through the peephole. "What can I do for you?"

"You can open the door and let me in to talk to your father," he growled. "Maybe he can explain what's been going on, since you won't."

"I told Mrs. Coombs all about it," Millie said. "She's a complete ass, making all this fuss about nothing."

"That's no way for a lady to talk, Millie," Mr. Tavistock said. "Especially an eleven-year-old. Open the door. I got a warrant."

He waved a paper in his huge hand.

"My father'll have you in court for trampling on his civil rights," Millie said. "I'll come to school tomorrow. I promise. But not today. My father mustn't be bothered."

"Let me in now, or we break the door down!" Mr. Tavistock shouted. "There's something funny going on, Millie, otherwise your father would've contacted the school long ago!"

"You people always think there's something funny about me, that's all!" Millie shouted back.

"Yeah, and Mrs. Coombs fell down over the wastebasket and wrenched her back right after she phoned you," Tavistock said. "Are you going to open that door?"

It would take them only a minute or so to kick the door open even if she chained it. She might as well let them in. Still, two more minutes might be all that were needed.

She reached for the knob and then dropped her hand. The typing had stopped.

She walked to the top of the basement steps.

"Pop! Are you through?"

She heard the squeaking of the swivel chair, then a shuffling sound. The house shook, and there was a crash as someone struck the front door with his body. A few seconds later, another crash was followed by the bang of the door against the inner wall. Mr. Tavistock said, "All right, boys! I'll lead the way!"

He sounded as if he were raiding a den of bank robbers, she thought.

She went around the corner to the front room and said, "I think my father is through."

"In more ways than one, Millie," Mr. Tavistock said.

She turned away and walked back around the corner, through the door and out onto the landing. Her father was standing at the bottom of the steps. His color was very bad and he looked as if he had gained much weight, though she knew that that was impossible.

He looked up at her from deeply sunken eyes, and he lifted the immense pile of sheets with his two hands.

"All done, Pop?" Millie said, her voice breaking.

He nodded slowly.

Millie heard the three men come up behind her. Mr. Tavistock leaned over her and said, "Whew!"

Millie turned and pushed at him. "Get out of my way! He's finished it!"

Mr. Tavistock glared, but he moved to one side. She walked to a chair and sat down heavily. One of the detectives said, "You look awful, Millie. You look like you haven't slept for a week."

"I don't think I'll ever be able to sleep," she said. She breathed deeply and allowed her muscles to go loose. Her head lolled as if she had given up control over everything inside her.

There was a thumping noise from the basement. Mr.

Tavistock cried out, "He's fainted!" The shoes of the three men banged on the steps as they ran down. A moment later Mr. Tavistock gave another cry. Then all three men began talking at once.

Millie closed her eyes and wished she could quit trembling. Some time later, she heard the footsteps. She did not want to open her eyes, but there was no use putting it off.

Mr. Tavistock was pale and shaking. He said, "My God! He looks, he smells like . . ."

One of the detectives said, "His fingertips are worn off, the bones are sticking out, but there wasn't any bleeding."

"I got him through," Millie said. "He finished it. That's all that counts."

Miss Thompson

♫ BY W. SOMERSET MAUGHAM

CHAPTER I

IT WAS nearly bedtime and when they awoke next morning land would be in sight.

Dr. Macphail lit his pipe and, leaning over the rail, searched the heavens for the Southern Cross. After two years at the front and a wound that had taken longer to heal than it should, he was glad to settle down quietly at Apia for twelve months at least, and he felt already better for the journey.

Since some of the passengers were leaving the ship next day at Pago-Pago they had had a little dance that evening and in his ears hammered still the harsh notes of the mechanical piano. But the deck was quiet at last. A little way off he saw his wife in a long chair talking with the Davidsons, and he strolled over to her. When he sat down under the light and took off his hat you saw that he had very red hair, with a bald patch on the crown, and the red, freckled skin which accompanies red hair; he was a man of forty, thin, with a pinched face, precise and rather pedantic and he spoke with a Scotch accent in a very low, quiet voice.

Between the Macphails and the Davidsons, who were missionaries, there had arisen the intimacy of shipboard, which is due to propinquity rather than to any community of taste. Their chief tie was the disapproval they shared of the men who spent their days and nights in the smoking room playing poker or bridge and drinking. Mrs. Macphail was not a little flattered to think that she and her husband were the only people on board with whom the Davidsons were willing to associate, and even the doctor, shy but no fool, half unconsciously acknowledged the compliment. It was only because he was of an argumentative mind that in their cabin at night he permitted himself to carp.

"Mrs. Davidson was saying she didn't know how they'd have got through the journey if it hadn't been for us," said Mrs. Macphail as she neatly brushed out her transformation. "She said we were really the only people on the ship they cared to know.'"

"I shouldn't have thought a missionary was such a big bug that he could afford to put on frills."

"It's not frills. I quite understand what she means. It wouldn't have been very nice for the Davidsons to have to mix with all that rough lot in the smoking room."

"The founder of their religion wasn't so exclusive," said Dr. Macphail with a chuckle.

"I've asked you over and over again not to joke about religion," answered his wife. "I shouldn't like to have a nature like yours, Alec. You never look for the best in people."

He gave her a sidelong glance with his pale, blue eyes, but did not reply. After many years of married life he had learned that it was more conducive to peace to leave his wife with the last word. He was undressed before her, and climbing into the upper bunk he settled down to read himself to sleep.

When he got on deck next morning they were close to the land. They ran along the island, and through his glasses he looked at it with greedy eyes. There was a thin strip of silver beach rising quickly to hills covered to the top with luxuriant vegetation. The coconut trees, thick and green, came nearly to the water's edge, and among them you saw the grass houses of the Samoans and here and there, gleaming white, a little church.

Mrs. Davidson came and stood beside him. She was dressed in black and wore round her neck a gold chain, from which dangled a small cross. She was a little woman, with brown, dull hair very elaborately arranged, and she had prominent blue eyes behind gold-rimmed pince-nez. Her face was long, like a sheep's, but she gave no impression of foolishness, rather of extreme alertness; she had the quick movements of a bird. The most remarkable thing about her was her voice, high, metallic, and without inflection; it fell on the ear with a hard monotony, irritating to the nerves like the pitiless clamour of a pneumatic drill.

"This must seem like home to you," said Dr. Macphail, with his thin, difficult smile.

"Ours are low islands, you know, not like these. Coral. These are volcanic. We've got another ten days' journey to reach them."

"In these parts that's almost like being in the next street at home," said Dr. Macphail facetiously.

"Well, that's rather an exaggerated way of putting it, but one does look at distances differently in the South Seas. So far you're right."

Dr. Macphail sighed faintly.

"I'm glad we're not stationed here," she went on. "They say this is a terribly difficult place to work in. The steamers touching make the people unsettled and then there's the naval station; that's bad for the natives. In our district we don't have difficulties like that to contend with. There are one or two traders, of course, but we take care to make them behave, and if they don't we make the place so hot for them they're glad to go."

Fixing the glasses on her nose she looked at the green island with a ruthless stare.

"It's almost a hopeless task for the missionaries here. I

can never be sufficiently thankful to God that we are at least spared that."

Davidson's district consisted of a group of islands to the north of Samoa; they were widely separated and he had frequently to go long distances by canoe. At these times his wife remained at their headquarters and managed the mission. Dr. Macphail felt his heart sink when he considered the efficiency with which she certainly managed it. She spoke of the depravity of the natives in a voice which nothing could hush, but with a vehemently unctuous horror. Her sense of delicacy was singular. Early in their acquaintance she had said to him:

"You know, their marriage customs when we first settled in the islands were so shocking that I couldn't possibly describe them to you. But I'll tell Mrs. Macphail and she'll tell you."

Then he had seen his wife and Mrs. Davidson, their deck chairs close together, in earnest conversation for about two hours. As he walked past them backwards and forwards for the sake of exercise he heard Mrs. Davidson's agitated whisper, like the distant flow of a mountain torrent, and he saw by his wife's open mouth and pale face that she was enjoying an alarming experience. At night in their cabin she repeated to him with bated breath all she had heard.

"Well, what did I say to you?" cried Mrs. Davidson, exultant next morning. "Did you ever hear anything more dreadful? You don't wonder that I couldn't tell you myself, do you? Even though you are a doctor."

Mrs. Davidson scanned his face. She had a dramatic eagerness to see that she had achieved the desired effect.

"Can you wonder that when we first went there our hearts sank? You'll hardly believe me when I tell you it was impossible to find a single good girl in any of the villages."

She used the word "good" in a severely technical manner.

"Mr. Davidson and I talked it over, and we made up our minds the first thing to do was to put down the dancing. The natives were crazy about dancing."

"I was not averse to it myself when I was a young man," said Dr. Macphail.

"I guessed as much when I heard you ask Mrs. Macphail to have a turn with you last night. I don't think there's any real harm if a man dances with his wife, but I was relieved that she wouldn't. Under the circumstances I thought it better that we should keep ourselves to ourselves."

"Under what circumstances?"

Mrs. Davidson gave him a quick look through her pince-nez, but did not answer his question.

"But among white people it's not quite the same," she went on, "though I must say I agree with Mr. Davidson, who says he can't understand how a husband can stand by and see his wife in another man's arms, and as far as I'm concerned I've never danced a step since I married. But the native dancing is quite another matter. It's not only immoral in itself, but it distinctly leads to immorality. However, I'm thankful to God that we stamped it out, and I don't think I'm wrong in saying that no one has danced in our district for eight years."

CHAPTER II

But now they came to the mouth of the harbor and Mrs. Macphail joined them. The ship turned sharply and steamed slowly in. It was a great landlocked harbour big enough to hold a fleet of battleships and all around it rose, high and steep, the green hills. Near the entrance, getting such breeze as blew from the sea, stood the Governor's house in a garden. The Stars and Stripes dangled languidly from a flagstaff. They passed two or three trim bungalows and a tennis court, and then they came to the quay with its warehouses.

Mrs. Davidson pointed out the schooner, moored two or three hundred yards from the side, which was to take them to Apia. There was a crowd of eager, noisy, and good-humoured natives come from all parts of the island, some from curiosity, others to barter with the travelers on their way to Sydney; and they brought pineapples and huge bunches of bananas, *tapa* cloths, necklaces of shells or shark's teeth, *kava* bowls, and models of war canoes. American sailors, neat and trim, clean-shaven and frank of face, sauntered among them, and there was a little group of officials.

While their luggage was being landed the Macphails and Mrs. Davidson watched the crowd. Dr. Macphail looked at the yaws from which most of the children and the young boys seemed to suffer, disfiguring chancres like torpid ulcers, and his professional eyes glistened when he saw for the first time in his experience cases of elephantiasis, men going about with a huge, heavy arm or dragging along a grossly disfigured leg. Men and women wore the *lava-lava*.

"It's a very indecent costume," said Mrs. Davidson.

"Mr. Davidson thinks it should be prohibited by law. How can you expect people to be moral when they wear nothing but a strip of red cotton round their loins?"

"It's suitable enough to the climate," said the doctor, wiping the sweat off his head.

Now that they were on land the heat, though it was so early in the morning, was already oppressive. Closed in by its hills, not a breath of air came in to Pago-Pago.

"In our islands," Mrs. Davidson went on in her high-pitched tones, "we've practically eradicated the *lava-lava*. A few old men still continue to wear it, but that's all. The women have all taken to the Mother Hubbard, and the men wear trousers and singlets. At the very beginning of our stay Mr. Davidson said in one of his reports: 'The inhabitants of these islands will never be thoroughly christianized till every boy of more than ten years is made to wear a pair of trousers.'"

But Mrs. Davidson had given two or three of her birdlike glances at heavy gray clouds that came floating over the mouth of the harbor. A few drops began to fall.

"We'd better take shelter," she said.

They made their way with all the crowd to a great shed of corrugated iron, and the rain began to fall in torrents. They stood there for some time and then were joined by Mr. Davidson. He had been polite enough to the Macphails during the journey, but he had not his wife's sociability, and had spent most of his time reading. He was a silent, rather sullen man, and you felt that his affability was a duty that he imposed upon himself christianly; he was by nature reserved and even morose.

His appearance was singular. He was very tall and thin, with long limbs loosely jointed; hollow cheeks and curiously high cheekbones; he had so cadaverous an air that it surprised you to notice how full and sensual were his lips. He wore his hair very long. His dark eyes, set deep in their sockets, were large and tragic; and his hands, with their big, long fingers, were finely shaped; they gave him a look of great strength. But the most striking thing about him was the feeling he gave you of suppressed fire. It was impressive and vaguely troubling. He was not a man with whom any intimacy was possible.

He brought now unwelcome news. There was an epidemic of measles, a serious and often fatal disease among the Kanakas, on the island, and a case had developed among the crew of the schooner which was to take them on their journey. The sick man had been brought ashore and put in hospital on the quarantine station, but telegraphic instructions had been sent from Apia to say that the schooner would not be allowed to enter the harbor till it was certain no other member of the crew was affected.

"It means we shall have to stay here for ten days at least."

"But I'm urgently needed at Apia," said Dr. Macphail.

"That can't be helped. If no more cases develop on board, the schooner will be allowed to sail with white passengers, but all native traffic is prohibited for three months."

"Is there a hotel here?" asked Mrs. Macphail.

Davidson gave a low chuckle.

"There's not."

"What shall we do then?"

"I've been talking to the Governor. There's a trader along the front who has rooms that he lets, and my proposition is that as soon as the rain lets up we should go along there and see what we can do. Don't expect comfort. You've just got to be thankful if we get a bed to sleep on and a roof over our heads."

But the rain showed no signs of stopping, and at length with umbrellas and waterproofs they set out. There was no town, but merely a group of official buildings, a store or two, and at the back, among the coconut trees and plantains, a few native dwellings. The house they sought was about five minutes' walk from the wharf. It was a frame house of two stories, with broad verandahs on both floors and a roof of corrugated iron.

The owner was a half-caste named Horn, with a native wife surrounded by little brown children, and on the ground floor he had a store where he sold canned goods and cottons. The rooms he showed them were almost bare of furniture. In the Macphails' there was nothing but a poor, worn bed with a ragged mosquito net, a rickety chair and a washstand. They looked around with dismay. The rain poured down without ceasing.

"I'm not going to unpack more than we actually need," said Mrs. Macphail.

Mrs. Davidson came into the room as she was unlocking a portmanteau. She was very brisk and alert. The cheerless surroundings had no effect on her.

"If you'll take my advice you'll get a needle and cotton and start right in to mend the mosquito net," she said, "or you'll not be able to get a wink of sleep tonight."

"Will they be very bad?" asked Dr. Macphail.

"This is the season for them. When you're asked to a party at Government House at Apia you'll notice that all the ladies are given a pillow slip to put their—their lower extremities in."

"I wish the rain would stop for a moment," said Mrs. Macphail. "I could try to make the place comfortable with more heart if the sun were shining."

"Oh, if you wait for that, you'll wait a long time. Pago-Pago is about the rainiest place in the Pacific. You see, the hills, and that bay, they attract the water, and one expects rain at this time of year anyway."

She looked from Macphail to his wife, standing helplessly in different parts of the room, like lost souls, and she pursed her lips. She saw that she must take them in hand. Feckless people like that made her impatient, but her hands itched to put everything in the order which came so naturally to her.

"Here, you give me a needle and cotton and I'll mend that net of yours, while you go on with your unpacking. Dinner's at one. Dr. Macphail, you'd better go down to the wharf and see that your heavy luggage has been put in a dry place. You know what these natives are. They're quite capable of storing it where the rain will beat in on it all the time."

Macphail put on his waterproof again and went downstairs. At the door the trader was standing in conversation with the quartermaster of the ship he had just arrived in and a second class passenger whom he had seen several times on board. The quartermaster, a little, shrivelled man, extremely dirty, nodded to him as he passed.

"This is a bad job about the measles, Doc," he said. "I see you've fixed yourself up already."

Dr. Macphail thought he was rather familiar, but he was a timid man and he did not take offense easily.

"Yes, we've got a room upstairs."

"Miss Thompson was sailing with you to Apia, so I've brought her along here."

The quartermaster pointed with his thumb to the woman standing by his side. She was twenty-seven perhaps, plump, and in a coarse fashion pretty. She wore a white dress and a large white hat. Her fat calves in white cotton stockings bulged over the tops of long white boots in glacé kid. She gave Macphail an ingratiating smile.

"The feller's tryin' to soak me a dollar and a half a day for the meanest sized room," she said in a hoarse voice.

"I tell you she's a friend of mine, Jo," said the quarter-master. "She can't pay more than a dollar, and you've sure got to take her for that."

The trader was fat and smooth and quietly smiling.

"Well, if you put it like that, Mr. Swan, I'll see what I can do about it. I'll talk to Mrs. Horn and if we think we can made a reduction we will."

"Don't try to pull that stuff with me," said Miss Thompson. "We'll settle this right now. You get a dollar a day for the room and not one bean more."

Dr. Macphail smiled. He admired the effrontery with which she bargained. He was the sort of man who always paid what he was asked. He preferred to be overcharged than to haggle. The trader sighed.

"Well, to oblige Mr. Swan I'll take it."

"That's the goods," said Miss Thompson. "Come right in and have a shot of hooch. I've got some real good rye in that grip if you'll bring it along, Mr. Swan. You come along too, Doctor."

"Oh, I don't think I will, thank you," he answered. "I'm just going down to see that our luggage is all right."

He stepped out into the rain. It swept in from the opening of the harbor in sheets and the opposite shore was all blurred. He passed two or three natives clad in nothing but the *lava-lava,* with huge umbrellas over them. They walked finely, with leisurely movements, very upright; and they smiled and greeted him in a strange tongue as they went by.

It was nearly dinner time when he got back, and their meal was laid in the trader's parlour. It was a room de-signed not to live in but for purposes of prestige, and it had a musty, melancholy air. A suite of stamped velvet was arranged neatly round the walls, and from the middle of the ceiling, protected from the flies by yellow tissue paper, hung a gilt chandelier. Davidson did not come.

"I know he went to call on the Governor," said Mrs. Davidson, "and I guess he's kept him to dinner."

A little native girl brought them a dish of Hamburger steak, and after a while the trader came up to see that they had everything they wanted.

"I see we have a fellow lodger, Mr. Horn," said Dr. Macphail.

"She's taken a room, that's all," answered the trader. "She's getting her own board."

He looked at the two ladies with an obsequious air.

"I put her downstairs so that she shouldn't be in the way. She won't be any trouble to you."

"Is it someone who was on the boat?" asked Mrs. Macphail.

"Yes, ma'am, she was in the second cabin. She was going to Apia. She has a position as cashier waiting for her."

"Oh!"

When the trader was gone Macphail said:

"I shouldn't think she'd find it exactly cheerful having her meals in her room."

"If she was in the second cabin I expect she'd rather," answered Mrs. Davidson. "I don't exactly know who it can be."

"I happened to be there when the quartermaster brought her along. Her name's Thompson."

"It's not the woman who was dancing with the quartermaster last night?" asked Mrs. Davidson.

"That's who it must be," said Mrs. Macphail. "I wondered at the time what she was. She looked rather fast to me."

"Not good style at all," said Mrs. Davidson.

CHAPTER III

They began to talk of other things, and after dinner, tired with their early rise, they separated and slept. When they awoke, though the sky was still gray and the clouds hung low, it was not raining and they went for a walk on the high road which the Americans had built along the bay.

On their return they found that Davidson had just come in.

"We may be here for a fortnight," he said irritably. "I've argued it out with the Governor, but he says there is nothing to be done."

"Mr. Davidson's just longing to get back to his work," said his wife with an anxious glance at him.

"We've been away for a year," he said, walking up and down the verandah. "The mission has been in charge of native missionaries and I'm terribly nervous that they've let things slide. They're good men, I'm not saying a word against them, God-fearing, devout and truly Christian men —their Christianity would put many so-called Christians at home to the blush—but they're pitifully lacking in energy. They can make a stand once, they can make a stand twice, but they can't make a stand all the time. If you leave a mission in charge of a native missionary, no matter how trustworthy he seems, in the course of time you'll find he's let abuses creep in."

Mr. Davidson stood still. With his tall, spare form, and his great eyes flashing out of his pale face, he was an impressive figure. His sincerity was obvious in the fire of his gestures and in his deep, ringing voice.

"I expect to have my work cut out for me. I shall act and I shall act promptly. If the tree is rotten it shall be cut down and cast into the flames."

And in the evening after the high tea which was their last meal, while they sat in the stiff parlour, the ladies working and Dr. Macphail smoking his pipe, the missionary told them of his work in the islands.

"When we went there they had no sense of sin at all," he said. "They broke the commandments one after the other and never knew they were doing wrong. And I think that was the most difficult part of my work—to instill into the natives the sense of sin."

The Macphails knew already that Davidson had worked

in the Solomons for five years before he met his wife. She had been a missionary in China, and they had become acquainted in Boston, where they were both spending part of their leave to attend a missionary congress. On their marriage they had been appointed to the islands in which they had labored ever since.

In the course of all the conversations they had had with Mr. Davidson one thing had shone out clearly and that was the man's unflinching courage. He was a medical missionary, and he was liable to be called at any time to one or other of the islands in the group. Even the whaleboat is not so very safe a conveyance in the stormy Pacific of the wet season, but often he would be sent for in a canoe and then the danger was great. In cases of illness or accident he never hesitated. A dozen times he had spent the whole night bailing for his life, and more than once Mrs. Davidson had given him up for lost.

"I'd beg him not to go sometimes," she said, "or at least to wait till the weather was more settled, but he'd never listen. He's obstinate, and when he's once made up his mind, nothing can move him."

"How can I ask the natives to put their trust in the Lord if I am afraid to do so myself?" cried Davidson. "And I'm not, I'm not. They know that if they send for me in their trouble, I'll come if it's humanly possible. And do you think the Lord is going to abandon me when I am on His business? The wind blows at His bidding and the waves toss and rage at His word."

Dr. Macphail was a timid man. He had never been able to get used to the hurtling of the shells over the trenches, and when he was operating in an advanced dressing station the sweat poured from his brow and dimmed his spectacles in the effort he made to control his unsteady hand. He shuddered a little as he looked at the missionary.

"I wish I could say that I've never been afraid," he said.

"I wish you could say that you believed in God," retorted the other.

But for some reason, that evening, the missionary's

thoughts travelled back to the early days he and his wife had spent on the islands.

"Sometimes Mrs. Davidson and I would look at one another and the tears would stream down our cheeks. We worked without ceasing, day and night, and we seemed to make no progress. I don't know what I should have done without her then. When I felt my heart sink, when I was very near despair, she gave me courage and hope."

Mrs. Davidson looked down at her work, and a slight color rose to her thin cheeks. Her hands trembled a little. She did not trust herself to speak.

"We had no one to help us. We were alone, thousands of miles from any of our own people, surrounded by darkness. When I was broken and weary she would put her work aside and take the Bible and read to me till peace came and settled upon me like sleep upon the eyelids of a child, and when at last she closed the book she'd say: 'We'll save them in spite of themselves.' And I felt strong again in the Lord and I answered, 'Yes, with God's help I'll save them. I *must* save them.'"

He came over to the table and stood in front of it as though it were a lectern.

"You see, they were so naturally depraved that they couldn't be brought to see their wickedness. We had to make sins out of what they thought were natural actions. We had to make it a sin, not only to commit adultery and to lie and thieve, but to expose their bodies, and to dance and not to come to church. I made it a sin for a girl to show her bosom and a sin for a man not to wear trousers."

"How?" asked Dr. Macphail, not without surprise.

"I instituted fines. Obviously the only way to make people realize that an action is sinful is to punish them if they commit it. I fined them if they didn't come to church, and I fined them if they danced. I fined them if they were improperly dressed. I had a tariff, and every sin had to be paid for either in money or work. And at last I made them understand."

"But did they never refuse to pay?"

"How could they?" asked the missionary.

"It would be a brave man who tried to stand up against Mr. Davidson," said his wife, tightening her lips.

Dr. Macphail looked at Davidson with troubled eyes. What he heard shocked him, but he hesitated to express his disapproval.

"You must remember that in the last resort I could expel them from their church membership."

"Did they mind that?"

Davidson smiled a little and gently rubbed his hands.

"They couldn't sell their copra. When the men fished they got no share of the catch. It meant something very like starvation. Yes, they minded quite a lot."

"Tell him about Fred Ohlson," said Mrs. Davidson.

The missionary fixed his fiery eyes on Dr. Macphail.

"Fred Ohlson was a Danish trader who had been in the islands a good many years. He was a pretty rich man as traders go and he wasn't very pleased when we came. You see, he'd had things very much his own way. He paid the natives what he liked for their copra, and he paid in goods and whisky. He had a native wife, but he was flagrantly unfaithful to her. He was a drunkard. I gave him a chance to mend his ways, but he wouldn't take it. He laughed at me."

Davidson's voice fell to a deep bass as he said the last words, and he was silent for a minute or two. The silence was heavy with menace.

"In two years he was a ruined man. He'd lost everything he'd saved in a quarter of a century. I broke him, and at last he was forced to come to me like a beggar and beseech me to give him a passage back to Sydney."

"I wish you could have seen him when he came to see Mr. Davidson," said the missionary's wife. "He had been a fine powerful man, with a lot of fat on him, and he had a great big voice, but now he was half the size, and he was shaking all over. He'd suddenly become an old man."

With abstracted gaze Davidson looked out into the night. The rain was falling again.

Suddenly from below came a sound, and Davidson turned and looked questioningly at his wife. It was the sound of a gramophone, harsh and loud, wheezing out a syncopated tune.

"What's that?" he asked.

Mrs. Davidson fixed her pince-nez more firmly on her nose.

"One of the second-class passengers has a room in the house. I guess it comes from there."

They listened in silence, and presently they heard the sound of dancing. Then the music stopped, and they heard the popping of corks and voices raised in animated conversation.

"I dare say she's giving a farewell party to her friends on board," said Dr. Macphail. "The ship sails at twelve, doesn't it?"

Davidson made no remark, but he looked at his watch.

"Are you ready?" he asked his wife.

She got up and folded her work.

"Yes, I guess I am," she answered.

"It's early to go to bed yet, isn't it?" said the doctor.

"We have a good deal of reading to do," explained Mrs. Davidson. "Wherever we are, we read a chapter of the Bible before retiring for the night and we study it with the commentaries, you know, and discuss it thoroughly. It's a wonderful training for the mind."

The two couples bade one another good night. Dr. and Mrs. Macphail were left alone. For two or three minutes they did not speak. "I think I'll go and fetch the cards," the doctor said at last.

Mrs. Macphail looked at him doubtfully. Her conversation with the Davidsons had left her a little uneasy, but she did not like to say that she thought they had better not play cards when the Davidsons might come in at any moment. Dr. Macphail brought them and she watched him though with a vague sense of guilt, while he laid out his patience. Below the sound of revelry continued.

CHAPTER IV

It was fine enough next day, and the Macphails, condemned to spend a fortnight of idleness at Pago-Pago, set about making the best of things.

They went down to the quay and got out of their boxes a number of books. The doctor called on the chief surgeon of the naval hospital and went round the beds with him. They left cards on the Governor. They passed Miss Thompson on the road. The doctor took off his hat, and she gave him a "Good morning, Doc!" in a loud, cheerful voice. She was dressed as on the previous day in a white frock, and her shiny white boots with their high heels, her fat legs bulging over the tops of them, were strange things in that primitive landscape.

"I don't think she's very suitably dressed, I must say," said Mrs. Macphail. "She looks extremely common to me."

When they got back to their house she was on the verandah playing with one of the trader's dark children.

"Say a word to her," Dr. Macphail whispered to his wife. "She's all alone here, and it seems rather unkind to ignore her."

Mrs. Macphail was shy, but she was in the habit of doing what her husband bade her.

"I think we're fellow lodgers here," she said, rather foolishly.

"Terrible, ain't it? Bein' cooped up in a one-horse place like this," answered Miss Thompson. "And they tell me I'm lucky to have gotten a room. I don't see myself livin' in a native house, and that's what some have to do. I don't know why they don't have a hotel."

They exchanged a few more words. Miss Thompson, loud-voiced and garrulous, was evidently quite willing to gossip, but Mrs. Macphail had a poor stock of small talk and presently she said:

"Well, I think we must go upstairs."

In the evening, when they sat down to their high tea, Davidson on coming in said:

"I see that woman downstairs has a couple of sailors sitting there. I wonder how she's gotten acquainted with them."

"She can't be very particular," said Mrs. Davidson.

They were all rather tired after the idle, aimless day.

"If there's going to be a fortnight of this I don't know what we shall feel like at the end of it," said Dr. Macphail.

"The only thing to do is to portion out the day to different activities," answered the missionary. "I shall set aside a certain number of hours to study and a certain number to exercise, rain or fine—in the wet season you can't afford to pay any attention to the rain—and a certain number to recreation."

Dr. Macphail looked at his companion with misgiving. Davidson's program oppressed him. They were eating Hamburger steak again. It seemed the only dish the cook knew how to make. Then below the gramophone began. Davidson started nervously when he heard it, but said nothing. Men's voices floated up. Miss Thompson's guests were joining in a well-known song and presently they heard her voice too, hoarse and loud. There was a good deal of shouting and laughing. The four people upstairs, trying to make conversation, listened despite themselves to the clink of glasses and the scrape of chairs. More people had evidently come. Miss Thompson was giving a party.

"I wonder how she gets them all in," said Mrs. Macphail, suddenly breaking into a medical conversation between the missionary and her husband.

It showed whither her thoughts were wandering. The twitch of Davidson's face proved that, though he spoke of scientific things, his mind was busy in the same direction. Suddenly, while the doctor was giving some experience of practice on the Flanders front, rather prosily, he sprang to his feet with a cry.

"What's the matter, Alfred?" asked Mrs. Davidson.

"Of course! It never occurred to me. She's out of Iwelei."

"She can't be."

"She came on board at Honolulu. It's obvious. And she's carrying on her trade here. Here!"

He uttered the last word with a passion of indignation.

"What's Iwelei?" asked Mrs. Macphail.

He turned his gloomy eyes on her and his voice trembled with horror.

"The plague spot of Honolulu. The Red Light district. It was a blot on our civilization."

Iwelei was on the edge of the city. You went down side streets by the harbor, in the darkness, across a rickety bridge till you came to a deserted road, all ruts and holes, and then suddenly you came out into the light. There was parking room for motors on each side of the road, and there were saloons, tawdry and bright, each one noisy with its mechanical piano, and there were barber shops and tobacconists. There was a stir in the air and a sense of expectant gaiety.

You turned down a narrow alley, either to the right or to the left, for the road divided Iwelei into two parts, and you found yourself in the district. There were rows of little bungalows, trim and neatly painted in green, and the pathway between them was broad and straight. It was laid out like a garden city. In its respectable regularity, its order and spruceness, it gave an impression of sardonic horror; for never can the search for love have been so systematized and ordered. The pathways were lit by a rare lamp, but they would have been dark except for the lights that came from the open windows of the bungalows.

Men wandered about, looking at the women who sat at their windows, reading or sewing, for the most part taking no notice of the passers-by; and like the women they were of all nationalities. There were Americans, sailors from the ships in port, enlisted men off the gunboats, sombrely drunk, and soldiers from the regiments, white and black, quartered on the island; there were Japanese, walking in twos and threes; Hawaiians, Chinese in long robes, and Filipinos in preposterous hats. They were silent and, as it were, oppressed. Desire is sad.

"It was the most crying scandal of the Pacific," exclaimed Davidson vehemently. "The missionaries had been agitating against it for years, and at last the local press took it up. The police refused to stir. You know their argument. They say that vice is inevitable and consequently the best thing is to localize and control it. The truth is, they were paid. Paid. They were paid by the saloon-keepers, paid by the bullies, paid by the women themselves. At last they were forced to move."

"I read about it in the papers that came on board in Honolulu," said Dr. Macphail.

"Iwelei, with its sin and shame, ceased to exist on the very day we arrived. The whole population was brought before the justices. I don't know why I didn't understand at once what that woman was."

"Now you come to speak of it," said Mrs. Macphail, "I remember seeing her come on board only a few minutes before the boat sailed. I remember thinking at the time she was cutting it rather fine."

"How dare she come here!" cried Davidson indignantly. "I'm not going to allow it."

He strode towards the door.

"What are you going to do?" asked Macphail.

"What do you expect me to do? I'm going to stop it. I'm not going to have this house turned into—into . . ." He sought for a word that should not offend the ladies' ears. His eyes were flashing and his pale face was paler still in his emotion.

"It sounds as though there were three or four men down there," said the doctor. "Don't you think it's rather rash to go in just now?"

The missionary gave him a contemptuous look and without a word flung out of the room.

"You know Mr. Davidson very little if you think the fear of personal danger can stop him in the performance of his duty," said his wife.

She sat with her hands nervously clasped, a spot of color on her high cheekbones, listening to what was about to happen below. They all listened.

They heard him clatter down the wooden stairs and throw open the door. The singing stopped suddenly, but the gramophone continued to bray out its vulgar tune. They heard Davidson's voice and then the noise of something heavy falling. The music stopped. He had hurled the gramophone on the floor. Then again they heard Davidson's voice, they could not make out the words, then Miss Thompson's, loud and shrill, then a confused clamor as though several people were shouting together at the top of their lungs.

Mrs. Davidson gave a little gasp, and she clenched her hands more tightly. Dr. Macphail looked uncertainly from her to his wife. He did not want to go down, but he wondered if they expected him to. Then there was something that sounded like a scuffle. The noise now was more distinct. It might be that Davidson was being thrown out of the room. The door was slammed. There was a moment's silence and they heard Davidson come up the stairs again. He went to his room.

"I think I'll go to him," said Mrs. Davidson.

She got up and went out.

"If you want me, just call," said Mrs. Macphail, and then when the other was gone, "I hope he isn't hurt."

"Why couldn't he mind his own business?" said Dr. Macphail.

They sat in silence for a minute or two and then they both started, for the gramophone began to play once more, defiantly, and mocking voices shouted hoarsely the words of an obscene song.

CHAPTER V

Next day Mrs. Davidson was pale and tired. She complained of headache, and she looked old and wizened. She told Mrs. Macphail that the missionary had not slept at all. He had passed the night in a state of frightful agitation and at five had got up and gone out. A glass of beer had been thrown over him and his clothes were stained and stinking. But a sombre fire glowed in Mrs. Davidson's eyes when she spoke of Miss Thompson.

"She'll bitterly rue the day when she flouted Mr. Davidson," she said. "Mr. Davidson has a wonderful heart and no one who is in trouble has ever gone to him without being comforted, but he has no mercy for sin, and when his righteous wrath is excited he's terrible."

"Why, what will he do?" asked Mrs. Macphail.

"I don't know, but I wouldn't stand in that creature's shoes for anything in the world."

Mrs. Macphail shuddered. There was something positively alarming in the triumphant assurance of the little woman's manner. They were going out together that morning, and they went down the stairs side by side. Miss Thompson's door was open, and they saw her in a bedraggled dressing gown, cooking something in a chafing dish.

"Good morning," she called. "Is Mr. Davidson better this morning?"

They passed her in silence, with their noses in the air, as if she did not exist. They flushed, however, when she burst into a shout of derisive laughter. Mrs. Davidson turned on her suddenly.

"Don't you dare to speak to me," she screamed. "If you insult me I shall have you turned out of here."

"Say, did I ask Mr. Davidson to call on me?"

"Don't answer her," whispered Mrs. Macphail hurriedly.

They walked on till they were out of earshot.

"She's brazen, brazen!" burst from Mrs. Davidson.

Her anger almost suffocated her.

And on their way home they met her strolling toward the quay. She had all her finery on. Her great white hat with its vulgar, showy flowers was an affront. She called out cheerily to them as she went by, and a couple of American sailors who were standing there grinned as the ladies set their faces to an icy stare. They got in just before the rain began to fall again.

"I guess she'll get her fine clothes spoilt," said Mrs. Davidson with a bitter sneer.

Davidson did not come in till they were halfway through dinner. He was wet through, but he would not change. He sat, morose and silent, refusing to eat more than a mouthful, and he stared at the slanting rain. When Mrs. Davidson told him of their two encounters with Miss Thompson he did not answer. His deepening frown alone showed that he had heard.

"Don't you think we ought to make Mr. Horn turn her out of here?" asked Mrs. Davidson. "We can't allow her to insult us."

"There doesn't seem to be any other place for her to go," said Macphail.

"She can live with one of the natives."

"In weather like this a native hut must be a rather uncomfortable place to live in."

"I lived in one for years," said the missionary.

When the little native girl brought in the fried bananas which formed the sweet they had every day, Davidson turned to her.

"Ask Miss Thompson when it would be convenient for me to see her," he said.

The girl nodded shyly and went out.

"What do you want to see her for, Alfred?" asked his wife.

"It's my duty to see her. I won't act till I've given her every chance."

"You don't know what she is. She'll insult you."

"Let her insult me. Let her spit on me. She has an immortal soul, and I must do all that is in my power to save it."

Mrs. Davidson's ears rang still with the harlot's mocking laughter.

"She's gone too far."

"Too far for the mercy of God?" His eyes lit up suddenly and his voice grew mellow and soft. "Never. The sinner may be deeper in sin than the depth of hell itself, but the love of the Lord Jesus can reach him still."

The girl came back with the message.

"Miss Thompson's compliments and as long as Rev. Davidson don't come in business hours she'll be glad to see him at any time."

The party received the message in stony silence, and Dr. Macphail quickly effaced from his lips the smile which had come upon them. He knew his wife would be vexed with him if he found Miss Thompson's effrontery amusing.

They finished the meal in silence. When it was over the two ladies got up and took their work—Mrs. Macphail was making another of the innumerable comforters which she had turned out since the beginning of the war—and the doctor lit his pipe. But Davidson remained in his chair and with abstracted eyes stared at the table.

At last he got up and without a word went out of the room. They heard him go down and they heard Miss Thompson's defiant "come in" when he knocked at the door. He remained with her for an hour. And Dr. Macphail watched the rain. It was beginning to get on his nerves. It was not like the soft English rain that drops gently on the earth, it was unmerciful and somehow terrible; you felt in it the malignancy of the primitive powers of nature. It did not pour, it flowed. It was like a deluge from heaven, and it rattled on the roof of corrugated iron with a steady persistence that was maddening. It seemed to have a fury of its own. And sometimes you felt that you must scream if it did not stop, and then suddenly you felt powerless, as though your bones had suddenly become soft, and you were miserable and hopeless.

Macphail turned his head when the missionary came back. The two women looked up.

"I've given her every chance. I have exhorted her to repent. She is an evil woman."

He paused, and Dr. Macphail saw his eyes darken and his pale face grow hard and stern.

"Now I shall take the whips with which the Lord Jesus drove the usurers and the moneychangers out of the temple of the Most High."

He walked up and down the room. His mouth was close set, and his black brows were frowning.

"If she fled to the uttermost parts of the earth I should pursue her."

With a sudden movement he turned round and strode out of the room. They heard him go downstairs again.

"What is he going to do?" asked Mrs. Macphail.

"I don't know." Mrs. Davidson took off her pince-nez and wiped them. "When he is on the Lord's work I never ask him questions."

She sighed a little.

"What is the matter?"

"He'll wear himself out. He doesn't know what it is to spare himself."

Dr. Macphail learnt the first results of the missionary's activity from the half-caste trader in whose house they lodged. He stopped the doctor when he passed the store and came out to speak to him on the stoop. His fat face was worried.

"The Rev. Davidson has been at me for letting Miss Thompson have a room here," he said, "but I didn't know what she was when I rented it to her. When people come and ask if I can rent them a room all I want to know is if they've the money to pay for it. And she paid me for hers a week in advance."

Dr. Macphail did not want to commit himself.

"When all's said and done it's your house. We're very much obliged to you for taking us in at all."

Horn looked at him doubtfully. He was not certain yet how definitely Macphail stood on the missionary's side.

"The missionaries are in with one another," he said hesitatingly. "If they get down on a trader he may just as well shut up his store and quit."

"Did he want you to turn her out?"

"No, he said so long as she behaved herself he couldn't ask me to do that. He said he wanted to be just to me. I promised she wouldn't have no more visitors. I've just been and told her."

"How did she take it?"

"She gave me hell."

The trader squirmed in his old ducks. He had found Miss Thompson a rough customer.

"Oh, well, I daresay she'll get out. I don't suppose she wants to stay here if she can't have anyone in."

"There's nowhere she can go, only a native house, and no native'll take her now, now that the missionaries have got their knife in her."

Dr. Macphail looked at the falling rain.

"Well, I don't suppose it's any good waiting for it to clear up."

In the evening when they sat in the parlor Davidson talked to them of his early days at college. He had had no means and had worked his way through by doing odd jobs during the vacations. There was silence downstairs. Miss Thompson was sitting in her little room alone.

But suddenly the gramophone began to play. She had set it on in defiance, to cheat her loneliness, but there was no one to sing, and it had a melancholy note. It was like a cry for help. Davidson took no notice. He was in the middle of a long anecdote and without change of expression he went on. The gramophone continued. Miss Thompson put on one record after another. It looked as if the silence of the night were getting on her nerves. It was breathless and sultry. When the Macphails went to bed they could not sleep. They lay side by side with their eyes wide open, listening to the cruel singing of the mosquitoes outside their curtain.

"What's that?" whispered Mrs. Macphail at last.

They heard a voice, Davidson's voice, through the wooden partition. It went on with a monotonous, earnest insistence. He was praying aloud. He was praying for the soul of Miss Thompson.

CHAPTER VI

Two or three days went by. Now when they passed Miss Thompson on the road she did not greet them with ironic cordiality or smile; she passed with her nose in the air, a sulky look on her painted face, frowning, as though she did not see them. The trader told Macphail that she had tried to get lodging elsewhere, but had failed.

In the evening she played through the various records of her gramophone, but the pretence of mirth was obvious now. The ragtime had a cracked, heartbroken rhythm as though it were a one-step of despair. When she began to play on Sunday Davidson sent Horn to beg her to stop at once since it was the Lord's Day. The record was taken off and the house was silent except for the steady pattering of the rain on the iron roof.

"I think she's getting a bit wrought up," said the trader next day to Macphail. "She don't know what Mr. Davidson's up to and it makes her scared."

Macphail had caught a glimpse of her that morning and it struck him that her arrogant expression had changed. There was in her face a hunted look. The half-caste gave him a sidelong glance.

"I suppose you don't know what Mr. Davidson is doing about it?" he hazarded.

"No, I don't."

It was singular that Horn should ask him that question, for he also had the idea that the missionary was mysteriously at work. He had an impression that he was weaving a net around the woman, carefully, systematically, and that suddenly, when everything was ready, he would pull the strings tight.

"He told me to tell her," said the trader, "that if at any time she wanted him she only had to send and he'd come."

"What did she say when you told her that?"

"She didn't say nothing. I didn't stop. I just said what he said I was to and then I beat it. I thought she might be going to start blubberin'."

"I have no doubt the loneliness is getting on her nerves," said the doctor. "And the rain—that's enough to make anyone jumpy," he continued irritably. "Doesn't it ever stop in this confounded place?"

"It goes on pretty steady in the rainy season. We have three hundred inches in the year. You see, it's the shape of the bay. It seems to attract the rain from all over the Pacific."

"Damn the shape of the bay," said the doctor.

He scratched his mosquito bites. He felt very short-tempered. When the rain stopped and the sun shone, it was like a hothouse, seething, humid, sultry, breathless, and you had a strange feeling that everything was growing with a savage violence. The natives, blithe and childlike by reputation, seemed then, with their tattooing and their dyed hair, to have something sinister in their appearance; and when they pattered along at your heels with their naked feet you looked back instinctively. You felt they might at any moment come behind you swiftly and thrust a long knife between your shoulder blades. You could not tell what dark thoughts lurked behind their wide-set eyes. They had a little the look of ancient Egyptians painted on a temple wall, and there was about them the terror of what is immeasurably old.

The missionary came and went. He was busy, but the Macphails did not know what he was doing. Horn told the doctor that he saw the Governor every day, and once Davidson mentioned him.

"He looks as if he had plenty of determination," he said, "but when you come down to brass tacks he has no backbone."

"I suppose that means he won't do exactly what you want," suggested the doctor facetiously.

The missionary did not smile.

"I want him to do what's right. It shouldn't be necessary to persuade a man to do that."

"But there may be differences of opinion about what is right."

"If a man had a gangrenous foot would you have patience with anyone who hesitated to amputate it?"

"Gangrene is a matter of fact."

"And Evil?"

What Davidson had done soon appeared. The four of them had just finished their midday meal, and they had not yet separated for the siesta which the heat imposed on the ladies and on the doctor. Davidson had little patience with the slothful habit. The door was suddenly flung open and Miss Thompson came in. She looked round the room and then went up to Davidson.

"You low-down skunk, what have you been saying about me to the Governor?"

She was spluttering with rage. There was a moment's pause. Then the missionary drew forward a chair.

"Won't you be seated, Miss Thompson? I've been hoping to have another talk with you."

"You poor low-life bastard!"

She burst into a torrent of insult, foul and insolent. Davidson kept his grave eyes on her.

"I'm indifferent to the abuse you think fit to heap on me, Miss Thompson," he said, "but I must beg you to remember that ladies are present."

Tears by now were struggling with her anger. Her face was red and swollen as though she were choking.

"What has happened?" asked Dr. Macphail.

"A feller's just been in here and he says I gotter beat it on the next boat."

Was there a gleam in the missionary's eyes? His face remained impassive.

"You could hardly expect him to let you stay here under the circumstances."

"You done it!" she shrieked. "You can't kid me. You done it!"

"I don't want to deceive you. I urged the Governor to take the only possible step consistent with his obligations."

"Why couldn't ye leave me be? I wasn't doin' you no harm."

"You may be sure that if you had I should be the last man to resent it."

"Do you think I want to stay on in this poor imitation of a burg? I don't look no busher, do I?"

"In that case I don't see what cause of complaint you have," he answered.

She gave an inarticulate cry of rage and flung out of the room. There was a short silence.

"It's a relief to know that the Governor has acted at last," said Davidson finally. "He's a weak man and he shilly-shallied. He said she was only here for a fortnight anyway, and if she went on to Apia that was under British jurisdiction and had nothing to do with him."

The missionary sprang to his feet and strode across the room.

"It's terrible the way the men who are in authority seek to evade their responsibility. They speak as though evil that was out of sight ceased to be evil. The very existence of that woman is a scandal and it does not help matters to shift it to another of the islands. In the end I had to speak straight from the shoulder."

Davidson's brow lowered, and he protruded his firm chin. He looked fierce and determined.

"What do you mean by that?"

"Our mission is not entirely without influence at Washington. I pointed out to the Governor that it wouldn't do him any good if there was a complaint about the way he managed things here."

"When has she got to go?" asked the doctor, after a pause.

"The San Francisco boat is due here from Sydney next Tuesday. She's to sail on that."

CHAPTER VII

That was in five days' time. It was next day, when he was coming back from the hospital where for want of something better to do Macphail spent most of his mornings, that the half-caste stopped him as he was going upstairs.

"Excuse me, Dr. Macphail, Miss Thompson's sick. Will you have a look at her?"

"Certainly."

Horn led him to her room. She was sitting in a chair idly, neither reading nor sewing, staring in front of her. She wore her white dress and the large hat with the flowers on it. Macphail noticed that her skin was yellow and muddy under her powder, and her eyes were heavy.

"I'm sorry to hear you're not well," he said.

"Oh, I ain't sick really. I just said that, because I just had to see you. I've got to clear on a boat that's going to Frisco."

She looked at him and he saw that her eyes were suddenly startled. She opened and clenched her hands spasmodically. The trader stood at the door, listening.

"So I understand," said the doctor.

She gave a little gulp.

"I guess it ain't very convenient for me to go to Frisco just now. I went to see the Governor yesterday afternoon, but I couldn't get to him. I saw the secretary, and he told me I'd got to take that boat and that was all there was to it. I just had to see the Governor, so I waited outside his house this morning, and when he come out I spoke to him. He didn't want to speak to me, I'll say, but I wouldn't let him shake me off, and at last he said he hadn't no objection to my staying here till the next boat to Sydney if the Rev. Davidson will stand for it."

She stopped and looked at Dr. Macphail anxiously.

"I don't know exactly what I can do," he said.

· "Well, I thought maybe you wouldn't mind asking him. I swear to God I won't start anything here if he'll just only let me stay. I won't go out of the house if that'll suit him. It's no more'n a fortnight."

"I'll ask him."

"He won't stand for it," said Horn. "He'll have you out on Tuesday, so you may as well make up your mind to it."

"Tell him I can get work in Sydney—straight stuff, I mean. 'Tain't asking very much."

"I'll do what I can."

"And come and tell me right away, will you? I can't set down to a thing till I get the dope one way or the other."

It was not an errand that much pleased the doctor, and, characteristically perhaps, he went about it indirectly. He told his wife what Miss Thompson had said to him and asked her to speak to Mrs. Davidson. The missionary's attitude seemed rather arbitrary and it could do no harm if the girl were allowed to stay in Pago-Pago another fortnight. But he was not prepared for the result of his diplomacy. The missionary came to him straightway.

"Mrs. Davidson tells me that Thompson has been speaking to you."

Dr. Macphail, thus directly tackled, had the shy man's resentment at being forced out into the open. He felt his temper rising, and he flushed.

"I don't see that it can make any difference if she goes to Sydney rather than to San Francisco, and so long as she promises to behave while she's here it's dashed hard to persecute her."

The missionary fixed him with his stern eyes.

"Why is she unwilling to go back to San Francisco?"

"I didn't inquire," answered the doctor with some asperity. "And I think one does better to mind one's own business."

Perhaps it was not a very tactful answer.

"The Governor has ordered her to be deported by the first boat that leaves the island. He's only done his duty and I will not interfere. Her presence is a peril here."

"I think you're very harsh and tyrannical."

The two ladies looked up at the doctor with some alarm, but they need not have feared a quarrel, for the missionary smiled gently.

"I'm terribly sorry you should think that of me, Dr. Macphail. Believe me, my heart bleeds for that unfortunate woman, but I'm only trying to do my duty."

The doctor made no answer. He looked out of the window sullenly. For once it was not raining and across the bay you saw nestling among the trees the huts of a native village.

"I think I'll take advantage of the rain stopping to go out," he said.

"Please don't bear me malice because I can't accede to your wish," said Davidson, with a melancholy smile. "I respect you very much, Doctor, and I should be sorry if you thought ill of me."

"I have no doubt you have a sufficiently good opinion of yourself to bear mine with equanimity," he retorted.

"That's one on me," chuckled Davidson.

When Dr. Macphail, vexed with himself because he had been uncivil to no purpose, went downstairs Miss Thompson was waiting for him with her door ajar.

"Well," she said, "have you spoken to him?"

"Yes. I'm sorry he won't do anything," he answered, not looking at her in his embarrassment.

But then he gave her a quick glance, for a sob broke from her. He saw that her face was white with fear. It gave him a shock of dismay. And suddenly he had an idea.

"But don't give up hope yet. I think it's a shame the way they're treating you and I'm going to see the Governor myself."

"Now?"

He nodded. Her face brightened.

"Say, that's real good of you. I'm sure he'll let me stay if you speak for me. I just won't do a thing I didn't ought all the time I'm here."

Dr. Macphail hardly knew why he had made up his mind to appeal to the Governor. He was perfectly indifferent to Miss Thompson's affairs, but the missionary had irritated him, and with him temper was a smouldering thing. He found the Governor at home. He was a large, handsome man, a sailor, with a gray toothbrush mustache; and he wore a spotless uniform of white drill.

"I've come to see you about a woman who's lodging in the same house as we are," he said. "Her name's Thompson."

"I guess I've heard nearly enough about her, Dr. Macphail," said the Governor, smiling. "I've given her the order to get out next Tuesday and that's all I can do."

"I wanted to ask you if you couldn't stretch a point and let her stay here till the boat comes in from San Francisco so that she can go to Sydney. I will guarantee her good behavior."

The Governor continued to smile, but his eyes grew small and serious.

"I'd be very glad to oblige you, Dr. Macphail, but I've given the order and it must stand."

The doctor put the case as reasonably as he could, but now the Governor ceased to smile at all. He listened sullenly, with averted gaze. Macphail saw that he was making no impression.

"I'm sorry to cause any lady inconvenience, but she'll have to sail on Tuesday and that's all there is to it."

"But what difference can it make?"

"Pardon me, Doctor, but I don't feel called upon to explain my official actions except to the proper authorities."

Macphail looked at him shrewdly. He remembered Davidson's hint that he had used threats, and in the Governor's attitude he read a singular embarrassment.

"Davidson's a damned busybody," he said hotly.

"Between ourselves, Dr. Macphail, I don't say that I have formed a very favorable opinion of Mr. Davidson, but I am bound to confess that he was within his rights in pointing out to me the danger that the presence of a woman of Miss

Thompson's character was to a place like this, where a number of enlisted men are stationed among a native population."

He got up and Dr. Macphail was obliged to do so, too.

"I must ask you to excuse me. I have an engagement. Please give my respects to Mrs. Macphail."

The doctor left him crestfallen. He knew that Miss Thompson would be waiting for him, and unwilling to tell her himself that he had failed, he went into the house by the back door and sneaked up the stairs as though he had something to hide.

CHAPTER VIII

At supper he was silent and ill-at-ease, but the missionary was jovial and animated. Dr. Macphail thought his eyes rested on him now and then with triumphant good humor.

It struck him suddenly that Davidson knew of his visit to the Governor and of its ill-success. But how on earth could he have heard of it? There was something sinister about the power of that man. After supper he saw Horn on the verandah and as though to have a casual word with him went out.

"She wants to know if you've seen the Governor," the trader whispered.

"Yes. He wouldn't do anything. I'm awfully sorry, I can't do anything more."

"I knew he wouldn't. They daren't go against the missionaries."

"What are you talking about?" said Davidson affably, coming out to join them.

"I was just saying there was no chance of your getting over to Apia for at least another week," said the trader glibly.

He left them, and the two men returned to the parlour. Mr. Davidson devoted one hour after each meal to recreation. Presently a timid knock was heard at the door.

"Come in," said Mrs. Davidson, in her sharp voice.

The door was not opened. She got up and opened it. They saw Miss Thompson standing at the threshold. But the change in her appearance was extraordinary. This was no longer the flaunting hussy who had jeered at them in the road, but a broken, frightened woman. Her hair, as a rule so elaborately arranged, was tumbling untidily over her neck. She wore bedroom slippers and a skirt and blouse. They were unfresh and bedraggled. She stood at the door with the tears streaming down her face and did not dare to come in.

"What do you want?" said Mrs. Davidson harshly.

"May I speak to Mr. Davidson?" she said in a choking voice.

The missionary rose and went toward her.

"Come right in, Miss Thompson," he said in cordial tones. "What can I do for you?"

She entered the room.

"Say, I'm sorry for what I said to you the other day an' for —for everythin' else. I guess I was a bit lit up. I beg pardon."

"Oh, it was nothing. I guess my back's broad enough to bear a few hard words."

She stepped toward him with a movement that was horribly cringing.

"You've got me beat. I'm all in. You won't make me go back to Frisco?"

His genial manner vanished and his voice grew on a sudden hard and stern.

"Why don't you want to go back there?"

She cowered before him.

"I guess my people live there. I don't want them to see me like this. I'll go anywhere else you say."

"Why don't you want to go back to San Francisco?"

"I've told you."

He leaned forward, staring at her, and his great, shining eyes seemed to try to bore into her soul. He gave a sudden gasp.

"The penitentiary."

She screamed, and then she fell at his feet, clasping his legs.

"Don't send me back there. I swear to you before God I'll be a good woman. I'll give all this up."

She burst into a torrent of confused supplication and the tears coursed down her painted cheeks. He leaned over her and lifting her face, forced her to look at him.

"Is that it, the penitentiary?"

"I beat it before they could get me," she gasped. "If the bulls grab me it's three years for mine."

He let go his hold of her and she fell in a heap on the floor, sobbing bitterly. Dr. Macphail stood up.

"This alters the whole thing," he said. "You can't make her go back when you know this. Give her another chance. She wants to turn over a new leaf."

"I'm going to give her the finest chance she's ever had. If she repents let her accept her punishment."

She misunderstood the words and looked up. There was a gleam of hope in her heavy eyes.

"You'll let me go?"

"No. You shall sail for San Francisco on Tuesday."

She gave a groan of horror and then burst into low, hoarse shrieks which sounded hardly human, and she beat her head passionately on the ground. Dr. Macphail sprang to her and lifted her up.

"Come on, you mustn't do that. You'd better go to your room and lie down. I'll get you something."

He raised her to her feet and partly dragging her, partly carrying her, got her downstairs. He was furious with Mr. Davidson and with his wife because they made no effort to help. The half-caste was standing on the landing and with his assistance he managed to get her on the bed. She was moaning and crying. She was almost insensible. He gave her a hypodermic injection. He was hot and exhausted when he went upstairs again.

"I've got her to lie down."

The two women and Davidson were in the same posi-

tions as when he had left them. They could not have moved
or spoken since he went.

"I was waiting for you," said Davidson, in a strange,
distant voice. "I want you all to pray with me for the soul of
our erring sister."

He took the Bible off a shelf, and sat down at the table at
which they had supped. It had not been cleared, and he
pushed the teapot out of the way. In a powerful voice,
resonant and deep, he read to them the chapter in which is
narrated the meeting of Jesus Christ with the woman
taken in adultery. Then he closed the book and went down
on his knees.

"Now kneel with me and let us pray for the soul of our
dear sister, Sadie Thompson."

He burst into a long, passionate prayer in which he im-
plored God to have mercy on the sinful woman. Mrs. Macphail and Mrs. Davidson knelt with covered eyes. The doctor, taken by surprise, awkward and sheepish, knelt too.
The missionary's prayer had a savage eloquence. He was
extraordinarily moved, and as he spoke the tears ran down
his cheeks. Outside, the pitiless rain fell, fell steadily, with
a fierce malignity that was all too human.

At last he stopped. He paused for a moment and said:

"We will now repeat the Lord's Prayer."

They said it and then, following him, they rose from
their knees. Mrs. Davidson's face was pale and restful. She
was comforted and at peace, but the Macphails felt suddenly bashful. They did not know which way to look.

"I'll just go down and see how she is now," said Dr.
Macphail.

When he knocked at her door it was opened for him by
Horn. Miss Thompson was in a rocking chair, sobbing
quietly.

"What are you doing there?" exclaimed Macphail. "I told
you to lie down."

"I can't lie down. I want to see Mr. Davidson."

"My poor child, what do you think is the good of it? You'll
never move him."

"He said he'd come if I sent for him."

Macphail motioned to the trader.

"Go and fetch him."

He waited with her in silence while the trader went upstairs. Davidson came in.

"Excuse me for asking you to come here," she said, looking at him sombrely.

"I was expecting you to send for me. I knew the Lord would answer my prayer."

They stared at one another for a moment and then she looked away. She kept her eyes averted when she spoke.

"I've been a bad woman. I want to repent."

"Thank God, thank God! He has heard our prayers."

He turned to the two men.

"Leave me alone with her. Tell Mrs. Davidson that our prayers have been answered."

They went out and closed the door behind them.

"Gee whizz!" said the trader.

That night Dr. Macphail could not get to sleep till late, and when he heard the missionary come upstairs he looked at his watch. It was two o'clock. But even then he did not go to bed at once, for through the wooden partition that separated their rooms he heard him praying aloud, till he himself, exhausted, fell asleep.

CHAPTER IX

When he saw him next morning he was surprised at his appearance. He was paler than ever, tired, but his eyes shone with an inhuman fire. It looked as though he were filled with an overwhelming joy.

"I want you to go down presently and see Sadie," he said. "I can't hope that her body is better, but her soul—her soul is transformed."

The doctor was feeling wan and nervous.

"You were with her very late last night," he said.

"Yes, she couldn't bear to have me leave her."

"You look as pleased as Punch," the doctor said irritably.

Davidson's eyes shone with ecstasy.

"A great mercy has been vouchsafed me. Last night I was privileged to bring a lost soul to the loving arms of Jesus."

Miss Thompson was again in the rocking chair. The bed had not been made. The room was in disorder. She had not troubled to dress herself, but wore a dirty dressing gown, and her hair was tied in a sluttish knot. She had given her face a dab with a wet towel, but it was all swollen and creased with crying. She looked drab.

She raised her eyes dully when the doctor came in. She was cowed and broken.

"Where's Mr. Davidson?" she asked.

"He'll come presently if you want him," answered Macphail, acidly. "I came here to see how you were."

"Oh, I guess I'm O.K. You needn't worry about that."

"Have you had anything to eat?"

"Horn brought me some coffee."

She looked anxiously at the door.

"D'you think he'll come down soon? I feel as if it wasn't so dreadful when he's with me."

"Are you still going on Tuesday?"

"Yes, he says I've got to go. Please tell him to come right along. You can't do me any good. He's the only one as can help me now."

"Very well," said Dr. Macphail.

During the next three days the missionary spent almost all his time with Sadie Thompson. He joined the others only to have his meals. Dr. Macphail noticed that he hardly ate.

"He's wearing himself out," said Mrs. Davidson pitifully. "He'll have a breakdown if he doesn't take care, but he won't spare himself."

She herself was white and pale. She told Mrs. Macphail that she had no sleep. When the missionary came upstairs from Miss Thompson he prayed till he was exhausted, but even then he did not sleep for long. After an hour or two he got up and dressed himself and went for a tramp along the bay. He had strange dreams.

"This morning he told me that he'd been dreaming about the mountains of Nebraska," said Mrs. Davidson.

"That's curious," said Dr. Macphail.

He remembered seeing them from the windows of the train when he crossed America. They were like huge mole-hills, rounded and smooth, and they rose from the plain abruptly. Dr. Macphail remembered how it struck him that they were like a woman's breasts.

Davidson's restlessness was intolerable even to himself. But he was buoyed up by a wonderful exhilaration. He was tearing out by the roots the last vestiges of sin that lurked in the hidden corners of that poor woman's heart. He read with her and prayed with her.

"It's wonderful," he said to them one day at supper. "It's a true rebirth. Her soul, which was black as night, is now pure and white like the new-fallen snow. I am humble and afraid. Her remorse for all her sins is beautiful. I am not worthy to touch the hem of her garment."

"Have you the heart to send her back to San Francisco?" said the doctor. "Three years in an American prison. I should have thought you might have saved her from that."

"Ah, but don't you see? It's necessary. Do you think my heart doesn't bleed for her? I love her as I love my wife and my sister. All the time that she is in prison I shall suffer all the pain that she suffers."

"Bunkum!" cried the doctor impatiently.

"You don't understand because you're blind. She's sinned, and she must suffer. I know what she'll endure. She'll be starved and tortured and humiliated. I want her to accept the punishment of man as a sacrifice to God. I want her to accept it joyfully. She has an opportunity which is offered to very few of us. God is very good and very merciful."

Davidson's voice trembled with excitement. He could hardly articulate the words that tumbled passionately from his lips.

"All day I pray with her and when I leave her I pray again, I pray with all my might and main, so that Jesus may grant her this great mercy. I want to put in her heart the passionate desire to be punished so that at the end, even if I offered to let her go she would refuse. I want her to feel that the bitter punishment of prison is the thank-offering that she places at the feet of our Blessed Lord, who gave His life for her."

The days passed slowly. The whole household, centered on the wretched, tortured woman downstairs, lived in a state of unnatural excitement. She was like a victim that was being prepared for the savage rites of a bloody idolatry. Her terror numbed her. She could not bear to let Davidson out of her sight. It was only when he was with her that she had courage, and she hung upon him with a slavish dependence. She cried a great deal, and she read the Bible, and prayed.

Sometimes she was exhausted and apathetic. Then she did indeed look forward to her ordeal, for it seemed to offer an escape, direct and concrete, from the anguish she was enduring. She could not bear much longer the vague terrors which now assailed her. With her sins she had put aside all personal vanity, and she slopped about her room, unkempt and dishevelled, in her tawdry dressing gown. She had not taken off her nightdress for four days, nor put on stockings. Her room was littered and untidy.

Meanwhile the rain fell with a cruel persistence. You felt that the heavens must at last be empty of water, but still it poured down, straight and heavy, with a maddening iteration on the iron roof. Everything was damp and clammy. There was mildew on the walls and on the boots that stood on the floor. Through the sleepless nights the mosquitoes droned their angry chant.

"If it would only stop raining for a single day it wouldn't be so bad," said Dr. Macphail.

They all looked forward to the Tuesday when the boat for San Francisco was to arrive from Sydney. The strain was intolerable. So far as Dr. Macphail was concerned, his pity and his resentment were alike extinguished by his desire to be rid of the unfortunate woman. The inevitable must be accepted. He felt he would breathe more freely when the ship had sailed. Sadie Thompson was to be escorted on board by a clerk in the Governor's office. This person called on the Monday evening and told Miss Thompson to be prepared at eleven in the morning. Davidson was with her.

"I'll see that everything is ready. I mean to come on board with her myself."

Miss Thompson did not speak.

When Dr. Macphail blew out his candle and crawled cautiously under his mosquito curtains, he gave a sigh of relief.

"Well, thank God that's over. By this time tomorrow she'll be gone."

"Mrs. Davidson will be glad, too. She says he's wearing himself to a shadow," said Mrs. Macphail. "She's a different woman."

"Who?"

"Sadie. I should never have thought it possible. It makes one humble."

Dr. Macphail did not answer, and presently he fell asleep. He was tired out, and he slept more soundly than usual.

CHAPTER X

He was awakened in the morning by a hand placed on his arm, and, starting up, saw Horn by the side of his bed. The trader put his finger on his mouth to prevent any exclamation from Dr. Macphail and beckoned to him to come.

As a rule he wore shabby ducks, but now he was barefoot and wore only the *lava-lava* of the natives. He looked suddenly savage, and Dr. Macphail, getting out of bed, saw that he was heavily tattooed. Horn made him a sign to come on to the verandah. Dr. Macphail got out of bed and followed the trader out.

"Don't make a noise," he whispered. "You're wanted. Put on a coat and some shoes. Quick."

Dr. Macphail's first thought was that something had happened to Miss Thompson.

"What is it? Shall I bring my instruments?"

"Hurry, please, hurry."

Dr. Macphail crept back into the bedroom, put on a waterproof over his pajamas, and a pair of rubber-soled shoes. He rejoined the trader, and together they tiptoed down the stairs. The door leading out to the road was open and at it were standing half a dozen natives.

"What is it?" repeated the doctor.

"Come along with me," said Horn.

He walked out and the doctor followed him. The natives came after them in a little bunch. They crossed the road and came on to the beach. The doctor saw a group of natives standing round some object at the water's edge. They hurried along, a couple of dozen yards perhaps, and the natives opened out as the doctor came up. The trader pushed him forward. Then he saw, lying half in the water and half out, a dreadful object, the body of Davidson.

Dr. Macphail bent down—he was not a man to lose his head in an emergency—and turned the body over. The throat was cut from ear to ear, and in the right hand was still the razor with which the deed was done.

"He's quite cold," said the doctor. "He must have been dead some time."

"One of the boys saw him lying there on his way to work just now and came and told me. Do you think he did it himself?"

"Yes. Someone ought to go for the police."

Horn said something in the native tongue, and two youths started off.

"We must leave him here till they come," said the doctor.

"They mustn't take him into my house. I won't have him in my house."

"You'll do what the authorities say," replied the doctor

sharply. "In point of fact I expect they'll take him to the mortuary."

They stood waiting where they were. The trader took a cigarette from a fold in his *lava-lava* and gave one to Dr. Macphail. They smoked while they stared at the corpse. Dr. Macphail could not understand.

"Why do you think he did it?" asked Horn.

The doctor shrugged his shoulders. In a little while native police came along, under the charge of a marine, with a stretcher, and immediately afterward a couple of naval officers and a naval doctor. They managed everything in a businesslike manner.

"What about the wife?" said one of the officers.

"Now that you've come I'll go back to the house and get some things on. I'll see that it's broken to her. She'd better not see him till he's been fixed up a little."

"I guess that's right," said the naval doctor.

When Dr. Macphail went back he found his wife nearly dressed.

"Mrs. Davidson's in a dreadful state about her husband," she said to him as soon as he appeared. "He hasn't been to bed all night. She heard him leave Miss Thompson's room at two, but he went out. If he's been walking about since then he'll be absolutely dead."

Dr. Macphail told her what had happened and asked her to break the news to Mrs. Davidson.

"But why did he do it?" she asked, horror-stricken.

"I don't know."

"But I can't. I can't."

"You must."

She gave him a frightened look and went out. He heard her go into Mrs. Davidson's room. He waited a minute to gather himself together and then began to shave and wash. When he was dressed he sat down on the bed and waited for his wife to come in again. At last she did.

"She wants to see him," she said.

"They've taken him to the mortuary. We'd better go down with her. How did she take it?"

"I think she's stunned. She didn't cry. But she's trembling like a leaf."

"We'd better go at once."

When they knocked at her door Mrs. Davidson came out. She was very pale, but dry-eyed. To the doctor she seemed unnaturally composed. No word was exchanged, and they set out in silence down the road. When they arrived at the mortuary Mrs. Davidson spoke.

"Let me go in and see him alone."

They stood aside. A native opened a door for her and closed it behind her. They sat down and waited in silence. One or two white men came and talked to them in undertones. Dr. Macphail told them again what he knew of the tragedy. At last the door was quietly opened and Mrs. Davidson came out. Silence fell upon them.

"I'm ready to go back now," she said.

Her voice was hard and steady. Dr. Macphail could not understand the look in her eyes. Her pale face was very stern. They walked back slowly, never saying a word, and at last they came round the bend, on the other side of which stood their house. Mrs. Davidson gave a gasp, and for a moment they stopped still. An incredible sound assaulted their ears. The gramophone which had been silent for so long was playing, playing ragtime loud and harsh.

"What's that?" cried Mrs. Macphail with horror.

"Let's go on," said Mrs. Davidson.

CHAPTER XI

They walked up the steps and entered the hall. Miss Thompson was standing at her door, chatting with a sailor.

A sudden change had taken place in her. She was no longer the cowed drudge of the last days. She was dressed in all her finery, in her white dress, with the high shiny boots over which her fat legs bulged in their cotton stockings; her hair was elaborately arranged; and she wore that enormous hat covered with gaudy flowers. Her face was painted, her eyebrows were boldly black, and her lips were scarlet. She held herself erect. She was the flaunting, impudent queen that they had known at first.

As they came in she broke into a loud, jeering laugh; and then, when Mrs. Davidson involuntarily stopped, she collected the spittle in her mouth and spat. Mrs. Davidson cowered back, and two red spots rose suddenly to her cheeks. Then, covering her face with her hands, she broke away and ran quickly up the stairs. Dr. Macphail was outraged. He pushed past the woman into her room.

"What the devil are you doing?" he cried. "Stop that damned machine."

He went up to it and tore the record off. She turned on him.

"Say, Doc, you can that stuff with me. What the hell are you doin' in my room?"

"What do you mean?" he cried. "What d'you mean?"

She gathered herself together. No one could describe the scorn of her expression or the contemptuous hatred she put into her answer.

"You men! You filthy, dirty pigs! You're all the same, all of you. Pigs! Pigs!"

Dr. Macphail gasped. He understood.

The Damnedest Thing

∮ BY GARSON KANIN

THE UNDERTAKER came home early. He kissed his wife, then went upstairs to wash up for supper. When he came down, *she* kissed *him*.

"Be five, six minutes," she said. "Legga lamb."

"Okay. I'll get me a drink," said the undertaker.

"And boiled leeks," she added, before returning to the kitchen.

The undertaker went into the sitting room and sat. Beside his chair, on a large end table, lay a copy of the evening paper. Beside it stood a nearly full bottle of whisky and a tumbler. He put the paper on his lap and smiled at the bottle as he would at a friend.

"Boy, oh, boy," he mumbled. He reached out and grasped the bottle firmly by its neck, keeping his thumb on the cork. He turned the bottle upside down once, then uncorked it. Next, he slowly decanted about two inches of liquor into the tumbler, corked the bottle, set it down, picked up the tumbler and drained it. He then put his nose into the empty glass and took one deep breath. Finally he put the glass beside the bottle and picked up his paper. His face was without expression as he scanned the top half of the front page, but when he flipped the paper over to look at the bottom half, a small headline took his attention, and he said to it quietly, "You don' say so!"

He returned the paper to his lap, reached out and grasped the bottle firmly by its neck, keeping his thumb on the cork. He turned the bottle upside down once, then uncorked it. Next, he slowly decanted about four inches of liquor into the tumbler, corked the bottle, set it down, picked up the tumbler and drained it. He then put his nose into the empty glass and took one deep breath. Finally he put the glass beside the bottle and picked up his paper. As he did so, his wife appeared in the archway which led to the dining room.

"Let's go," she said. "Everything's on."

"Right there," he replied, and made his way to his place at the table. His wife was already seated at hers, piling food onto her plate. He reached to the platter of lamb and served himself, meagerly.

His wife bristled. "What's the matter? Against lamb?"

"No."

"Then so what?"

"I think I just killed off my whole appetite."

"Why?"

"I didn't mean it, only I did. With an extry slug of whisky."

"What'd you want t'do *that* for?"

"I didn't *want*, I just *did*. A double slug, if you want the truth."

"You'da told me in time, I coulda saved myself in the kitchen, Arthur. Far as I'm personally concerned, delicatessen suits me as soon as lamb."

"I didn't know I was going to."

"How about tomorrow *you* cook a legga lamb and *I'll* get crocked an' not eat? Why not?"

"Don' make a situation, Rhoda. I said I'm sorry."

"When? I didn' hear no sorry."

"All right. I'm saying it now. Sorry."

"You're welcome."

They ate in silence, until Arthur ended it. "Good piece of meat. Gristede's?"

"A lot you know. Drunk."

He put down his fork. "Rhoda, I want to assure you this much. That I'm not drunk. Far from it. In fact, I wish we had the habit of a glass of wine with meals. Red, white, I don' know which it is you're supposed to with lamb. But in the store, they prob'ly give a free booklet. It's a nice habit to have. Very civilized. In many countries they wouldn't think of without it. And got nothing to do with drunk in any way, shape, manner or form." He picked up his fork and resumed the meal.

"If I knew what's got into you all of a sudden," said Rhoda, "I would be happy. I'm always telling how at least you, whatever faults you got, don't make a pig of yourself when it comes to alcoholic beverage. You've always been strictly moderation. Practice and preach."

"I'm *still.*"

"So what's all this extry slugs and you want suddenly wine in addition?"

"The wine I just happened to mention. A civilized habit."

"An' the extry slugs?"

"Slug, not *slugs."*

"So *slug?"*

"That's something else again."

"What else again?"

"Rhoda, if you knew the thing happened to me today, you absolutely wouldn' begrudge me."

"I don't begrudge, Arthur. I like you to have anything in the world if you want it. Only I worry if I see you turning into like Gunderson over there with nothing in his stomach only rye whisky and prunes for a year an' two months, Mrs. Gunderson tells me." She munched her food sadly.

"Rhoda, I advise you put your mind at rest. With all my faults, as you mentioned—an' one of these days, by the way, if I get the time I appreciate you telling me just what you call faults; not now, though—one of them is not I'm alcoholic or even nearly. The wine talk was one thing, just a topic of conversation, figure of speech, y'might say. The other thing, the extry slug—not *slugs, slug*—this is something else again. This I admit to, in fact, brought up myself. An' the reason was what happened to me today down to the place. When I tell you, if I tell you, you will definitely not begrudge me. In fact, take a slug yourself, I wouldn' be surprised. Only I don' know should I tell you."

"Tell, don' tell," chanted Rhoda.

"It was the damnedest thing ever happened to me in my entire life. In fact, *God* damnedest," said the undertaker.

"Eat your meat."

"Rhoda, listen. Because this is it." He took a breath and swallowed before continuing. "I had an argument with a corpse today."

"Eat a few vegetables, at least, if not meat."

"Did you hear what I just told?"

"Yes."

"Well, there's more. Not only I had this argument with this corpse, but I *lost* the argument, what's more."

"The feature goes on seven-ten," replied Rhoda. "But if you wanna catch the newsreel an' cartoon, then ten *to.* "

"I just as soon."

"All right, then, don't dawdle. Salad?"

"Yes. Look, I can't seem to put my point over. Oh! You think I'm affected by the—but no, Rhoda. I take an oath, I raise my hand. I know what I'm talking of and this is the God's truth what I'm on the verge to tell you."

"All right, Arthur. But eat meanwhile."

"Now the stiff I had the run-in with, the corpse, is Stanton C. Baravale. Was."

"The department store."

"That's him. Last night he died, in the private wing of Summit General. Ten-fifty-three P.M."

"I read it, yes."

"This morning they brought him in early; in fact, they were waiting out front when I got there."

"Because you got a late start, I told you. You wanna watch that."

"You're one hundred percent wrong, Rhoda, but I got no time to argue because I don' want to lose my thread. So they brought him in and we laid him out careful in the big room, and just about we were getting ready to go to work, Thor says to me, 'Mr. Roos, could I be excused?' "

"I like to see you excuse him for good," said Rhoda. "That dope."

"No, he's a good boy. But he says further, 'I slammed out with no breakfast an' I like to go to the Whelan's get a bite to eat.' 'Go ahead,' I says, 'only I hope no trouble home.' So Thor tells me how again his mother starts on him regarding learning the embalming game. How it makes her nervous he's an embalmer's apprentice. Some people!"

"How'd she like it there was *nobody* doin' the type work?"

"The very point I made to Thor, darling."

"An' what'd *he* say?"

"That it was the very point he made to *her.*"

"I should think so, f'God's sake!"

"Anyway, he goes to the Whelan's, an' I start in gettin' the stuff prepared. An' I was whistling, I remember well, because I was whistling 'There Is Nothing Like a Dame' an' I was havin' trouble to recall the middle part which slipped my mind."

"Ta da da *da* da da *da!*" sang Rhoda, helpfully.

"Yes, I know. It came to me later. But while I was whistling, I heard this noise. Like the clearing of a throat. Well, I turned."

"An' what was it?" asked Rhoda, interested for the first time.

"It was the clearing of a throat."

"What're you saying, Arthur?"

"I'm saying that Stanton C. Baravale was sitting up, looking terrible sick."

"Why shouldn't he if he was dead?"

"Wait a second, Rhoda. Let me get on with it. The man sat there an' he looks at me, then he looks around, then to me, then he says—but soft, he was so soft I could hardly hear 'im. Like this. He says, 'Who're you?' "

Rhoda stacked their plates, pushed them aside, pulled the pie tin toward her and began cutting it, carefully.

"Arthur, are you telling the truth?"

"As God is my judge."

"Then go ahead," said Rhoda. "Only speak up while I get the coffee off."

"In twenty-eight years," shouted Arthur, "it's happened to me twice only. The other time, you remember, the Winkleman boy how he came to in the shop an' it was in all the papers, an' he's still around, I believe. Since nineteen twenty-eight."

Rhoda returned with the coffeepot, sat down and poured two cups.

"He's still around," she said, "and a very mean job he turned out. All the time in trouble."

"So when Stanton C. Baravale said, 'Who're you?' like that, I told him. Naturally. An' where he was, an' he asks me how come. So I said, 'Well, the fact is, Mr. Baravale, you died last night. Ten-fifty-three P.M.' 'I knew it must be *something* like that,' he says. 'I feel light as a feather. An' cold, too,' he says. 'I must have a temperature of below zero.' So I says, 'You just relax, sir, an' I'll get Summit General on the phone in one second.' 'Don't do that,' he says. 'It'll just cause talk, an' I'm goin' out again in a minute.' "

"Think of that," said Rhoda, sipping her boiling coffee.

"Darling," continued the undertaker, "I want to tell you, I just stood there. I was in a state of shock. Next thing, he was talkin' again. 'What was it?' he says, still whisperin', y'know. 'There was something worryin' me I didn't settle, that's why I came back. I know,' he says, a little louder. *'You!'* "

"You?" echoed Rhoda.

"That's it. He says to me how like a fool he never specified any burial details, an' just left it general. That it was the last thing he was thinkin' about before he went off, an' some kind of leftover power in his brain must've brought him back for long enough."

"Arthur, I don't begrudge you that extry slug. Not for one moment."

" 'Now then,' he says to me, 'what's it going to cost?' 'I really couldn't say,' I says. 'You better,' he says. 'The way that fool Immerman drew the damn thing it reads "after all funeral expenses have been paid," and so forth. Well, hell,' he says, 'that can mean *anything.* Moment like this, my kids feel bad, they're bound to spend more'n is necessary, and what's the sense to that? Now what's the cheapest?' he says. 'All depends,' I answer him, 'how many persons, cars, music or no, casket.' At this he leans on his elbow an' he says, 'Six people, one car, no music, cheapest box you carry.' So I says, 'But what if the instructions I get—' He never let me finish. 'God damn it,' he says. 'Give me some paper an' pen'n ink.' I give it him, he writes a page, then he says, 'You have any trouble, show that!' Well, Rhoda, by this time I was comin' to *myself* a little more. An' I says, 'Please let me use the phone.' 'No,' he says, 'just give me your gentleman's word you'll handle it my way.' 'But, look,' I says, 'this paper's no good. You're legally dead as of ten-fifty-three P.M. last night.' 'That's why I put last week's date on,' he says. 'An' it's in my handwriting, no mistake about that.' Then he says to me, 'What's the time *now?'* 'Eight-thirteen A.M.,' I says. 'Well, let's make it eight-fifteen, officially,' he says, and lays down again and says the date. 'January five, nineteen fifty-six,' he says. 'Thank you, Mr. Roos,' he says. 'Been nice talkin' to you.' An' then, Rhoda, he just by God went out!"

"Well, I never," said Rhoda. "Gimme a hand here, will you, Arthur, please?"

Together they cleared the table, replaced the lace centerpiece and the wax-fruit bowl. In the kitchen, he washed, she dried. They worked for a time with swift efficiency, without speaking. Finally Rhoda asked, "What're you goin' t'do?"

"Y'got me there, dear."

"You mentioned to anyone? Thor?"

"Not yet, no."

"They ordered up anything yet?"

"Doggone right. Man brought a letter from the lawyer's place. Big chapel, minimum three hundred guests. Organ *and* string trio. Thirty cars. Canopy and chairs. Memorial reception after, main hall. Organ *and* string trio. Refreshments. Rhoda, one of the biggest things we've ever handled. I mean it's between seven, eight hundred clear profit no matter how you look."

"You got the page he wrote there?"

"Right here," said Arthur.

"Lemme have a look it."

"Wait'll I wipe my hands here." Having dried his hands, he took the paper from his breast pocket and handed it to his wife.

She read it carefully. "Well," she said. "Only one thing to do."

"That's right," said Arthur. "You want to or me?"

"I'll," said Rhoda, stepping to the gas range.

"Careful, dear," cautioned Arthur. "Don't burn yourself."

"No, darling," said his wife. She turned on the gas jet nearest her. The automatic monitor ignited the burner and Rhoda held a corner of the paper over it. She turned the jet off as the paper began to burn, neatly. Holding it before her she crossed the kitchen to the sink and joined her husband. Now she carefully placed the flaming handful in the sink. They both stood there, watching the paper turn to ash. Arthur put his arm around his wife, tenderly.

"It's not like he couldn't spare it," he said.

"An' anyways," added Rhoda, "why cheat family and friends from paying proper last respects?"

"—crossed my mind, too," said Arthur.

"Furthermore, he had no right to do what he did."

"None whatsoever," agreed Arthur. "A man legally dead, after all."

"You know where we're gonna sit tonight?" asked Rhoda.

"Loges."

"Yes. Costly, but smoking."

In the sink, the flame died. Rhoda slapped at the black ash, lightly, with her forefinger. Arthur turned on the faucet. Suddenly the sink was clear.

The undertaker and his wife washed their hands together and went to the movies. They arrived in time to see not only the newsreel and the cartoon, but Coming Attractions as well.

De Mortuis

❡ BY JOHN COLLIER

DR. RANKIN was a large and rawboned man on whom the newest suit at once appeared outdated, like a suit in a photograph of twenty years ago. This was due to the squareness and flatness of his torso, which might have been put together by a manufacturer of packing cases. His face also had a wooden and a roughly constructed look; his hair was wiglike and resentful of the comb. He had those huge and clumsy hands which can be an asset to a doctor in a small upstate town where people still retain a rural relish for paradox, thinking that the more apelike the paw, the more precise it can be in the delicate business of a tonsillectomy.

This conclusion was perfectly justified in the case of Dr. Rankin. For example, on this particular fine morning, though his task was nothing more ticklish than the cementing over of a large patch on his cellar floor, he managed those large and clumsy hands with all the unflurried certainty of one who would never leave a sponge within or create an unsightly scar without.

The Doctor surveyed his handiwork from all angles. He added a touch here and a touch there till he had achieved

91

a smoothness altogether professional. He swept up a few last crumbs of soil and dropped them into the furnace. He paused before putting away the pick and shovel he had been using, and found occasion for yet another artistic sweep of his trowel, which made the new surface precisely flush with the surrounding floor. At this moment of supreme concentration the porch door upstairs slammed with the report of a minor piece of artillery, which, appropriately enough, caused Dr. Rankin to jump as if he had been shot.

The Doctor lifted a frowning face and an attentive ear. He heard two pairs of heavy feet clump across the resonant floor of the porch. He heard the house door opened and the visitors enter the hall, with which his cellar communicated by a short flight of steps. He heard whistling and then the voices of Buck and Bud crying, "Doc! Hi, Doc! They're biting!"

Whether the Doctor was not inclined for fishing that day, or whether, like others of his large and heavy type, he experienced an especially sharp, unsociable reaction on being suddenly startled, or whether he was merely anxious to finish undisturbed the job in hand and proceed to more important duties, he did not respond immediately to the inviting outcry of his friends. Instead, he listened while it ran its natural course, dying down at last into a puzzled and fretful dialogue.

"I guess he's out."

"I'll write a note—say we're at the creek, to come on down."

"We could tell Irene."

"But she's not here, either. You'd think *she'd* be around."

"Ought to be, by the look of the place."

"You said it, Bud. Just look at this table. You could write your name—"

"Sh-h-h! Look!"

Evidently the last speaker had noticed that the cellar

door was ajar and that a light was shining below. Next moment the door was pushed wide open and Bud and Buck looked down.

"Why, Doc! There you are!"

"Didn't you hear us yelling?"

The Doctor, not too pleased at what he had overheard, nevertheless smiled his rather wooden smile as his two friends made their way down the steps. "I thought I heard someone," he said.

"We were bawling our heads off," Buck said. "Thought nobody was home. Where's Irene?"

"Visiting," said the Doctor. "She's gone visiting."

"Hey, what goes on?" said Bud. "What are you doing? Burying one of your patients, or what?"

"Oh, there's been water seeping up through the floor," said the Doctor. "I figured it might be some spring opened up or something."

"You don't say!" said Bud, assuming instantly the high ethical standpoint of the realtor. "Gee, Doc, I sold you this property. Don't say I fixed you up with a dump where there's an underground spring."

"There was water," said the Doctor.

"Yes, but, Doc, you can look on that geological map the Kiwanis Club got up. There's not a better section of subsoil in the town."

"Looks like he sold you a pup," said Buck, grinning.

"No," said Bud. "Look. When the Doc came here he was green. You'll admit he was green. The things he didn't know!"

"He bought Ted Webber's jalopy," said Buck.

"He'd have bought the Jessop place if I'd let him," said Bud. "But I wouldn't give him a bum steer."

"Not the poor, simple city slicker from Poughkeepsie," said Buck.

"Some people would have taken him," said Bud. "Maybe some people did. Not me. I recommended this property. He and Irene moved straight in as soon as they were married.

I wouldn't have put the Doc on to a dump where there'd be a spring under the foundations."

"Oh, forget it," said the Doctor, embarrassed by this conscientiousness. "I guess it was just the heavy rains."

"By gosh!" Buck said, glancing at the besmeared point of the pickax. "You certainly went deep enough. Right down into the clay, huh?"

"That's four feet down, the clay," Bud said.

"Eighteen inches," said the Doctor.

"Four feet," said Bud. "I can show you on the map."

"Come on. No arguments," said Buck. "How's about it, Doc? An hour or two at the creek, eh? They're biting."

"Can't do it, boys," said the Doctor. "I've got to see a patient or two."

"Aw, live and let live, Doc," Bud said. "Give 'em a chance to get better. Are you going to depopulate the whole darn town?"

The Doctor looked down, smiled, and muttered, as he always did when this particular jest was trotted out. "Sorry, boys," he said. "I can't make it."

"Well," said Bud, disappointed, "I suppose we'd better get along. How's Irene?"

"Irene?" said the Doctor. "Never better. She's gone visiting. Albany. Got the eleven o'clock train."

"Eleven o'clock?" said Buck. "For Albany?"

"Did I say Albany?" said the Doctor. "Watertown, I meant."

"Friends in Watertown?" Buck asked.

"Mrs. Slater," said the Doctor. "Mr. and Mrs. Slater. Lived next door to 'em when she was a kid, Irene said, over on Sycamore Street."

"Slater?" said Bud. "Next door to Irene. Not in *this* town."

"Oh, yes," said the Doctor. "She was telling me all about them last night. She got a letter. Seems this Mrs. Slater looked after her when her mother was in the hospital one time."

"No," said Bud.

"That's what she told me," said the Doctor. "Of course, it was a good many years ago."

"Look, Doc," said Buck. "Bud and I were raised in this town. We've known Irene's folks all our lives. We were in and out of their house all the time. There was never anybody next door called Slater."

"Perhaps," said the Doctor, "she married again, this woman. Perhaps it was a different name."

Bud shook his head.

"What time did Irene go to the station?" Buck asked.

"Oh, about a quarter of an hour ago," said the Doctor.

"You didn't drive her?" said Buck.

"She walked," said the Doctor.

"We came down Main Street," Buck said. "We didn't meet her."

"Maybe she walked across the pasture," said the Doctor.

"That's a tough walk with a suitcase," said Buck.

"She just had a couple of things in a little bag," said the Doctor.

Bud was still shaking his head.

Buck looked at Bud, and then at the pick, at the new, damp cement on the floor. "Jesus Christ!" he said.

"Oh, God, Doc!" Bud said. "A guy like you!"

"What in the name of heaven are you two bloody fools thinking?" asked the Doctor. "What are you trying to say?"

"A spring!" said Bud. "I ought to have known right away it wasn't any spring."

The Doctor looked at his cement work, at the pick, at the large worried faces of his two friends. His own face turned livid. "Am I crazy?" he said. "Or are you? You suggest that I've—that Irene—my wife—oh, go on! Get out! Yes, go and get the sheriff. Tell him to come here and start digging. You —get out!"

Bud and Buck looked at each other, shifted their feet, and stood still again.

"Go on," said the Doctor.

"I don't know," said Bud.

"It's not as if he didn't have the provocation," Buck said.

"God knows," Bud said.

"God knows," Buck said. "You know. I know. The whole town knows. But try telling it to a jury."

The Doctor put his hand to his head. "What's that?" he said. "What is it? Now what are you saying? What do you mean?"

"If this ain't being on the spot!" said Buck. "Doc, you can see how it is. It takes some thinking. We've been friends right from the start. Damn good friends."

"But we've got to think," said Bud. "It's serious. Provocation or not, there's a law in the land. There's such a thing as being an accomplice."

"You were talking about provocation," said the Doctor.

"You're right," said Buck. "And you're our friend. And if ever it could be called justified—"

"We've got to fix this somehow," said Bud.

"Justified?" said the Doctor.

"You were bound to get wised up sooner or later," said Buck.

"We could have told you," said Bud. "Only—what the hell?"

"We could," said Buck. "And we nearly did. Five years ago. Before ever you married her. You hadn't been here six months, but we sort of cottoned to you. Thought of giving you a hint. Spoke about it. Remember, Bud?"

Bud nodded. "Funny," he said. "I came right out in the open about that Jessop property. I wouldn't let you buy that, Doc. But getting married, that's something else again. We could have told you."

"We're that much responsible," Buck said.

"I'm fifty," said the Doctor. "I suppose it's pretty old for Irene."

"If you was Johnny Weissmuller at the age of twenty-one, it wouldn't make any difference," said Buck.

"I know a lot of people think she's not exactly a perfect wife," said the Doctor. "Maybe she's not. She's young. She's full of life."

"Oh, skip it!" said Buck sharply, looking at the raw cement. "Skip it, Doc, for God's sake."

The Doctor brushed his hand across his face. "Not everybody wants the same thing," he said. "I'm a sort of dry fellow. I don't open up very easily. Irene—you'd call her gay."

"You said it," said Buck.

"She's no housekeeper," said the Doctor. "I know it. But that's not the only thing a man wants. She's enjoyed herself."

"Yeah," said Buck. "She did."

"That's what I love," said the Doctor. "Because I'm not that way myself. She's not very deep, mentally. All right. Say she's stupid. I don't care. Lazy. No system. Well, I've got plenty of system. She's enjoyed herself. It's beautiful. It's innocent. Like a child."

"Yes. If that was all," Buck said.

"But," said the Doctor, turning his eyes full on him, "you seem to know there was more."

"Everybody knows it," said Buck.

"A decent, straightforward guy comes to a place like this and marries the town floozy," Bud said bitterly. "And nobody'll tell him. Everybody just watches."

"And laughs," said Buck. "You and me, Bud, as well as the rest."

"We told her to watch her step," said Bud. "We warned her."

"Everybody warned her," said Buck. "But people get fed up. When it got to truck drivers—"

"It was never us, Doc," said Bud, earnestly. "Not after you came along, anyway."

"The town'll be on your side," said Buck.

"That won't mean much when the case comes to trial in the county seat," said Bud.

"Oh!" cried the Doctor, suddenly. "What shall I do? What shall I do?"

"It's up to you, Bud," said Buck. "I can't turn him in."

"Take it easy, Doc," said Bud. "Calm down. Look, Buck.

When we came in here the street was empty, wasn't it?"

"I guess so," said Buck. "Anyway, nobody saw us come down cellar."

"And we haven't been down," Bud said, addressing himself forcefully to the Doctor. "Get that, Doc? We shouted upstairs, hung around a minute or two, and cleared out. But we never came down into this cellar."

"I wish you hadn't," the Doctor said heavily.

"All you have to do is say Irene went out for a walk and never came back," said Buck. "Bud and I can swear we saw her headed out of town with a fellow in a—well, say in a Buick sedan. Everybody'll believe that, all right. We'll fix it. But later. Now we'd better scram."

"And remember, now. Stick to it. We never came down here and we haven't seen you today," said Bud. "So long!"

Buck and Bud ascended the steps, moving with a rather absurd degree of caution. "You'd better get that . . . that thing covered up," Buck said over his shoulder.

Left alone, the Doctor sat down on an empty box, holding his head with both hands. He was still sitting like this when the porch door slammed again. This time he did not start. He listened. The house door opened and closed. A voice cried, "Yoo-hoo! Yoo-hoo! I'm back."

The Doctor rose slowly to his feet. "I'm down here, Irene!" he called.

The cellar door opened. A young woman stood at the head of the steps. "Can you beat it?" she said. "I missed the damn train."

"Oh!" said the Doctor. "Did you come back across the field?"

"Yes, like a fool," she said. "I could have hitched a ride and caught the train up the line. Only I didn't think. If you'd run me over to the junction, I could still make it."

"Maybe," said the Doctor. "Did you meet anyone coming back?"

"Not a soul," she said. "Aren't you finished with that old job yet?"

"I'm afraid I'll have to take it all up again," said the Doctor. "Come down here, my dear, and I'll show you."

Tobermory

BY SAKI

It was a chill, rain-washed afternoon of a late August day, that indefinite season when partridges are still in security or cold storage, and there is nothing to hunt—unless one is bounded on the north by the Bristol Channel, in which case one may lawfully gallop after fat red stags. Lady Blemley's house party was not bounded on the north by the Bristol Channel, hence there was a full gathering of her guests round the tea table on this particular afternoon. And, in spite of the blankness of the season and the triteness of the occasion, there was no trace in the company of that fatigued restlessness which means a dread of the pianola and a subdued hankering for auction bridge. The undisguised open-mouthed attention of the entire party was fixed on the homely negative personality of Mr. Cornelius Appin. Of all her guests, he was the one who had come to Lady Blemley with the vaguest reputation. Someone had said he was "clever," and he had got his invitation in the moderate expectation, on the part of his hostess, that some portion at least of his cleverness would be contributed to the general entertainment. Until teatime that day she had been unable to discover in what direction, if any, his cleverness lay. He was neither a wit nor a croquet champion, a hypnotic force nor a begetter of amateur theatricals. Neither did his exterior suggest the sort of man in whom women are willing to pardon a generous measure of mental deficiency. He had subsided into mere Mr. Appin, and the Cornelius seemed a piece of transparent baptismal bluff. And now he was claiming to have launched on the world a discovery beside which the invention of gunpowder, of the printing press, and of steam locomotion were inconsiderable trifles. Science had made bewildering strides in many directions during recent decades, but this thing seemed to belong to the domain of miracle rather than to scientific achievement.

"And do you really ask us to believe," Sir Wilfrid was saying, "that you have discovered a means for instructing animals in the art of human speech, and that dear old Tobermory has proved your first successful pupil?"

"It is a problem at which I have worked for the last seventeen years," said Mr. Appin, "but only during the last eight or nine months have I been rewarded with glimmerings of success. Of course I have experimented with thousands of animals, but latterly only with cats, those wonderful creatures which have assimilated themselves so marvelously with our civilization while retaining all their highly developed feral instincts. Here and there among cats one comes across an outstanding superior intellect, just as one does among the ruck of human beings, and when I made the acquaintance of Tobermory a week ago I saw at once that I was in contact with a 'Beyond-cat' of extraordinary intelligence. I had gone far along the road to success in recent experiments; with Tobermory, as you call him, I have reached the goal."

Mr. Appin concluded his remarkable statement in a voice which he strove to divest of a triumphant inflection. No one said "Rats," though Clovis's lips moved in a monosyllabic contortion which probably invoked those rodents of disbelief.

"And do you mean to say," asked Miss Resker, after a slight pause, "that you have taught Tobermory to say and understand easy sentences of one syllable?"

"My dear Miss Resker," said the wonder worker patiently, "one teaches little children and savages and backward adults in that piecemeal fashion; when one has once solved the problem of making a beginning with an animal of highly developed intelligence one has no need for those halting methods. Tobermory can speak our language with perfect correctness."

This time Clovis very distinctly said, "Beyond-rats!" Sir Wilfrid was more polite, but equally sceptical.

"Hadn't we better have the cat in and judge for ourselves?" suggested Lady Blemley.

Sir Wilfrid went in search of the animal, and the company settled themselves down to the languid expectation of witnessing some more or less adroit drawing-room ventriloquism.

In a minute Sir Wilfrid was back in the room, his face white beneath its tan and his eyes dilated with excitement.

"By Gad, it's true!"

His agitation was unmistakably genuine, and his hearers started forward in a thrill of awakened interest.

Collapsing into an armchair he continued breathlessly: "I found him dozing in the smoking room, and called out to him to come for his tea. He blinked at me in his usual way, and I said, 'Come on, Toby; don't keep us waiting; and, by Gad! he drawled out in a most horribly natural voice that he'd come when he dashed well pleased! I nearly jumped out of my skin!"

Appin had preached to absolutely incredulous hearers; Sir Wilfrid's statement carried instant conviction. A Babel-like chorus of startled exclamation arose, amid which the scientist sat mutely enjoying the first fruit of his stupendous discovery.

In the midst of the clamor Tobermory entered the room and made his way with velvet tread and studied unconcern across to the group seated round the tea table.

A sudden hush of awkwardness and constraint fell on the company. Somehow there seemed an element of embarrassment in addressing on equal terms a domestic cat of acknowledged mental ability.

"Will you have some milk, Tobermory?" asked Lady Blemley in a rather strained voice.

"I don't mind if I do," was the response, couched in a tone of even indifference. A shiver of suppressed excitement went through the listeners, and Lady Blemley might be excused for pouring out the saucerful of milk rather unsteadily.

"I'm afraid I've spilt a good deal of it," she said apologetically.

"After all, it's not my Axminster," was Tobermory's rejoinder.

Another silence fell on the group, and then Miss Resker, in her best district-visitor manner, asked if the human language had been difficult to learn. Tobermory looked squarely at her for a moment and then fixed his gaze serenely on the middle distance. It was obvious that boring questions lay outside his scheme of life.

"What do you think of human intelligence?" asked Mavis Pellington lamely.

"Of whose intelligence in particular?" asked Tobermory coldly.

"Oh, well, mine for instance," said Mavis, with a feeble laugh.

"You put me in an embarrassing position," said Tobermory, whose tone and attitude certainly did not suggest a shred of embarrassment. "When your inclusion in this house party was suggested Sir Wilfrid protested that you were the most brainless woman of his acquaintance, and that there was a wide distinction between hospitality and the care of the feeble-minded. Lady Blemley replied that your lack of brain power was the precise quality which had earned you your invitation, as you were the only person she could think of who might be idiotic enough to buy their old car. You know, the one they call 'The Envy of Sisyphus,' because it goes quite nicely uphill if you push it."

Lady Blemley's protestations would have had greater effect if she had not casually suggested to Mavis only that morning that the car in question would be just the thing for her down at her Devonshire home.

Major Barfield plunged in heavily to effect a diversion.

"How about your carryings-on with the tortoise-shell puss up at the stables, eh?"

The moment he had said it every one realized the blunder.

"One does not usually discuss these matters in public," said Tobermory frigidly. "From a slight observation of your ways since you've been in this house I should imagine you'd find it inconvenient if I were to shift the conversation on to your own little affairs."

The panic which ensued was not confined to the Major.

"Would you like to go and see if cook has got your dinner ready?" suggested Lady Blemley hurriedly, affecting to ignore the fact that it wanted at least two hours to Tobermory's dinnertime.

"Thanks," said Tobermory, "not quite so soon after my tea. I don't want to die of indigestion."

"Cats have nine lives, you know," said Sir Wilfrid heartily.

"Possibly," answered Tobermory; "but only one liver."

"Adelaide!" said Mrs. Cornett, "do you mean to encourage that cat to go out and gossip about us in the servants' hall?"

The panic had indeed become general. A narrow ornamental balustrade ran in front of most of the bedroom windows at the Towers, and it was recalled with dismay that this had formed a favorite promenade for Tobermory at all hours, whence he could watch the pigeons—and heaven knew what else besides. If he intended to become reminiscent in his present outspoken strain the effect would be something more than disconcerting. Mrs. Cornett, who spent much time at her toilet table, and whose complexion was reputed to be of a nomadic though punctual disposition, looked as ill at ease as the Major. Miss Scrawen, who wrote fiercely sensuous poetry and led a blameless life, merely displayed irritation; if you are methodical and virtuous in private you don't necessarily want everyone to know it. Bertie van Tahn, who was so depraved at seventeen that he had long ago given up trying to be any worse, turned a dull shade of gardenia white, but he did not commit the error of dashing out of the room like Odo Finsberry, a young gentleman who was understood to be reading for the Church and who was possibly disturbed at the thought of scandals he might hear concerning other people. Clovis had the presence of mind to maintain a composed exterior; privately he was calculating how long it would take to procure a box of fancy mice through the agency of the *Exchange and Mart* as a species of hush money.

Even in a delicate situation like the present, Agnes Resker could not endure to remain too long in the background.

"Why did I ever come down here?" she asked dramatically.

Tobermory immediately accepted the opening.

"Judging by what you said to Mrs. Cornett on the croquet lawn yesterday, you were out for food. You described the Blemleys as the dullest people to stay with that you knew, but said they were clever enough to employ a first-rate cook; otherwise they'd find it difficult to get any one to come down a second time."

"There's not a word of truth in it! I appeal to Mrs. Cornett—" exclaimed the discomfited Agnes.

"Mrs. Cornett repeated your remark afterwards to Bertie van Tahn," continued Tobermory, "and said, 'That woman is a regular Hunger Marcher; she'd go anywhere for four square meals a day,' and Bertie van Tahn said—"

At this point the chronicle mercifully ceased. Tobermory had caught a glimpse of the big yellow tom from the Rectory working his way through the shrubbery towards the stable wing. In a flash he had vanished through the open French window.

With the disappearance of his too-brilliant pupil Cornelius Appin found himself beset by a hurricane of bitter upbraiding, anxious inquiry, and frightened entreaty. The responsibility for the situation lay with him, and he must prevent matters from becoming worse. Could Tobermory impart his dangerous gift to other cats? was the first question he had to answer. It was possible, he replied, that he might have initiated his intimate friend the stable puss into his new accomplishment, but it was unlikely that his teaching could have taken a wider range as yet.

"Then," said Mrs. Cornett, "Tobermory may be a valuable cat and a great pet; but I'm sure you'll agree, Adelaide, that both he and the stable cat must be done away with without delay."

"You don't suppose I've enjoyed the last quarter of an hour, do you?" said Lady Blemley bitterly. "My husband and I are very fond of Tobermory—at least, we were before this horrible accomplishment was infused into him; but now, of course, the only thing is to have him destroyed as soon as possible."

"We can put some strychnine in the scraps he always gets at dinnertime," said Sir Wilfrid, "and I will go and drown the stable cat myself. The coachman will be very sore at losing his pet, but I'll say a very catching form of mange has broken out in both cats and we're afraid of it spreading to the kennels."

"But my great discovery!" expostulated Mr. Appin; "after all my years of research and experiment—"

"You can go and experiment on the shorthorns at the farm, who are under proper control," said Mrs. Cornett, "or the elephants at the Zoological Gardens. They're said to be highly intelligent, and they have this recommendation, that they don't come creeping about our bedrooms and under chairs, and so forth."

An archangel ecstatically proclaiming the millennium, and then finding that it clashed unpardonably with Henley and would have to be indefinitely postponed, could hardly have felt more crestfallen than Cornelius Appin at the reception of his wonderful achievement. Public opinion, however, was against him—in fact, had the general voice been consulted on the subject it is probable that a strong minority vote would have been in favor of including him in the strychnine diet.

Defective train arrangements and a nervous desire to see matters brought to a finish prevented an immediate dispersal of the party, but dinner that evening was not a social success. Sir Wilfrid had had rather a trying time with the stable cat and subsequently with the coachman. Agnes Resker ostentatiously limited her repast to a morsel of dry toast, which she bit as though it were a personal enemy; while Mavis Pellington maintained a vindictive silence throughout the meal. Lady Blemley kept up a flow of what she hoped was conversation, but her attention was fixed on the doorway. A plateful of carefully dosed fish scraps was in readiness on the sideboard, but sweets and savory and dessert went their way, and no Tobermory appeared either in the dining room or kitchen.

The sepulchral dinner was cheerful compared with the subsequent vigil in the smoking room. Eating and drinking had at least supplied a distraction and cloak to the prevailing embarrassment. Bridge was out of the question in the general tension of nerves and tempers, and after Odo Finsberry had given a lugubrious rendering of "Mélisande in the Wood" to a frigid audience, music was tacitly avoided. At eleven the servants went to bed, announcing that the small window in the pantry had been left open as usual for Tobermory's private use. The guests read steadily through the current batch of magazines, and fell back gradually on the "Badminton Library" and bound volumes of *Punch*.

Lady Blemley made periodic visits to the pantry, returning each time with an expression of listless depression which forestalled questioning.

At two o'clock Clovis broke the dominating silence.

"He won't turn up tonight. He's probably in the local newspaper office at the present moment, dictating the first installment of his reminiscences. Lady What's-her-name's book won't be in it. It will be the event of the day."

Having made this contribution to the general cheerfulness, Clovis went to bed. At long intervals the various members of the house party followed his example.

The servants taking round the early tea made a uniform announcement in reply to a uniform question. Tobermory had not returned.

Breakfast was, if anything, a more unpleasant function than dinner had been, but before its conclusion the situation was relieved. Tobermory's corpse was brought in from the shrubbery, where a gardener had just discovered it. From the bites on his throat and the yellow fur which coated his claws it was evident that he had fallen in unequal combat with the big tom from the Rectory.

By midday most of the guests had quitted the Towers, and after lunch Lady Blemley had sufficiently recovered her spirits to write an extremely nasty letter to the Rectory about the loss of her valuable pet.

Tobermory had been Appin's one successful pupil, and he was destined to have no successor. A few weeks later an elephant in the Dresden Zoological Garden, which had shown no previous signs of irritability, broke loose and killed an Englishman who had apparently been teasing it. The victim's name was variously reported in the papers as Oppin and Eppelin, but his front name was faithfully rendered Cornelius.

"If he was trying German irregular verbs on the poor beast," said Clovis, "he deserved all he got."

Undertaker Song

𝕤 BY DAMON RUNYON

Now this story I am going to tell you is about the game of
football, a very healthy pastime for the young, and a great
character-builder from all I hear, but to get around to this
game of football I am compelled to bring in some most
obnoxious characters, beginning with a guy by the name
of Joey Perhaps, and all I can conscientiously say about
Joey is you can have him.

It is a matter of maybe four years since I see this Joey
Perhaps until I notice him on a train going to Boston, Mass.,
one Friday afternoon. He is sitting across from me in the
dining car, where I am enjoying a small portion of baked
beans and brown bread, and he looks over to me once, but
he does not rap to me.

There is no doubt but what Joey Perhaps is bad company,
because the last I hear of him he is hollering copper on a
guy by the name of Jack Ortega, and as a consequence of
Joey Perhaps hollering copper, this Jack Ortega is taken to
the city of Ossining, N. Y., and placed in an electric chair,
and given a very, very, very severe shock in the seat of his
pants.

It is something about plugging a most legitimate business guy in the city of Rochester, N. Y., when Joey Perhaps and Jack Ortega are engaged together in a little enterprise to shake the guy down, but the details of this transaction are dull, and sordid, and quite uninteresting, except that Joey Perhaps turns state's evidence and announces that Jack Ortega fires the shot which cools the legitimate guy off, for which service he is rewarded with only a small stretch.

I must say for Joey Perhaps that he looks good, and he is very well dressed, but then Joey is always particular about clothes, and he is quite a handy guy with the dolls in his day and, to tell the truth, many citizens along Broadway are by no means displeased when Joey is placed in the state institution, because they are generally pretty uneasy about their dolls when he is around.

Naturally, I am wondering why Joey Perhaps is on this train going to Boston, Mass., but for all I know maybe he is wondering the same thing about me, although I am making no secret about it. The idea is I am en route to Boston, Mass., to see a contest of skill and science that is to take place there this very Friday night between a party by the name of Lefty Ledoux and another party by the name of Mickey McCoy, who are very prominent middleweights.

Now ordinarily I will not go around the corner to see a contest of skill and science between Lefty Ledoux and Mickey McCoy, or anybody else, as far as that is concerned, unless they are using blackjacks and promise to hurt each other, but I am the guest on this trip of a party by the name of Meyer Marmalade, and will go anywhere to see anything if I am a guest.

This Meyer Marmalade is really a most superior character, who is called Meyer Marmalade because nobody can ever think of his last name, which is something like Marmalodowski, and he is known far and wide for the way he likes to make bets on any sporting proposition, such as baseball, or horse races, or ice hockey, or contests of skill and science, and especially contests of skill and science.

So he wishes to be present at this contest in Boston, Mass., between Lefty Ledoux and Mickey McCoy to have a nice wager on McCoy, as he has reliable information that McCoy's manager, a party by the name of Koons, has both judges and the referee in the satchel.

If there is one thing Meyer Marmalade dearly loves, it is to have a bet on a contest of skill and science of this nature, and so he is going to Boston, Mass. But Meyer Marmalade is such a guy as loathes and despises traveling all alone, so when he offers to pay my expenses if I will go along to keep him company, naturally I am pleased to accept, as I have nothing on of importance at the moment and, in fact, I do not have anything on of importance for the past ten years.

I warn Meyer Marmalade in advance that if he is looking to take anything off of anybody in Boston, Mass., he may as well remain at home, because everybody knows that statistics show that the percentage of anything being taken off of the citizens of Boston, Mass., is less per capita than anywhere else in the United States, especially when it comes to contests of skill and science, but Meyer Marmalade says this is the first time they ever had two judges and a referee running against the statistics, and he is very confident.

Well, by and by I go from the dining car back to my seat in another car, where Meyer Marmalade is sitting reading a detective magazine, and I speak of seeing Joey Perhaps to him. But Meyer Marmalade does not seem greatly interested, although he says to me like this:

"Joey Perhaps, eh?" he says. "A wrong gee. A dead wrong gee. He must just get out. I run into the late Jack Ortega's brother, young Ollie, in Mindy's restaurant last week," Meyer Marmalade says, "and when we happen to get to talking of wrong gees, naturally Joey Perhaps' name comes up, and Ollie remarks he understands Joey Perhaps is about due out, and that he will be pleased to see him some day. Personally," Meyer Marmalade says, "I do not care for any part of Joey Perhaps at any price."

Now our car is loaded with guys and dolls who are going

to Boston, Mass., to witness a large football game between the Harvards and the Yales at Cambridge, Mass., the next day, and the reason I know this is because they are talking of nothing else.

So this is where the football starts getting into this story.

One old guy that I figure must be a Harvard from the way he talks seems to have a party all his own, and he is getting so much attention from one and all in the party that I figure he must be a guy of some importance, because they laugh heartily at his remarks, and although I listen very carefully to everything he says he does not sound so very humorous to me.

He is a heavy-set guy with a bald head and a deep voice, and anybody can see that he is such a guy as is accustomed to plenty of authority. I am wondering out loud to Meyer Marmalade who the guy can be, and Meyer Marmalade states as follows:

"Why," he says, "he is nobody but Mr. Phillips Randolph, who makes the automobiles. He is the sixth richest guy in this country," Meyer says, "or maybe it is the seventh. Anyway, he is pretty well up with the front runners. I spot his monicker on his suitcase, and then I ask the porter, to make sure. It is a great honor for us to be traveling with Mr. Phillips Randolph," Meyer says, "because of him being such a public benefactor and having so much dough, especially having so much dough."

Well, naturally everybody knows who Mr. Phillips Randolph is, and I am surprised that I do not recognize his face myself from seeing it so often in the newspapers alongside the latest model automobile his factory turns out, and I am as much pleasured up as Meyer Marmalade over being in the same car with Mr. Phillips Randolph.

He seems to be a good-natured old guy, at that, and he is having a grand time, what with talking, and laughing, and taking a dram now and then out of a bottle, and when old Crip McGonnigle comes gimping through the car selling his football souvenirs, such as red and blue feathers, and little badges, and pennants, and one thing and another, as Crip is doing around the large football games since Hickory Slim is a two-year-old, Mr. Phillips Randolph stops him and buys all of Crip's red feathers, which have a little white H on them to show they are for the Harvards.

Then Mr. Phillips Randolph distributes the feathers around among his party, and the guys and dolls stick them in their hats, or pin them on their coats, but he has quite a number of feathers left over, and about this time who comes through the car but Joey Perhaps, and Mr. Phillips Randolph steps out in the aisle and stops Joey and politely offers him a red feather, and speaks as follows:

"Will you honor us by wearing our colors?"

Well, of course Mr. Phillips Randolph is only full of good spirits, and means no harm whatever, and the guys and dolls in his party laugh heartily as if they consider his action very funny, but maybe because they laugh, and maybe because he is just naturally a hostile guy, Joey Perhaps knocks Mr. Phillips Randolph's hand down, and says like this:

"Get out of my way," Joey says. "Are you trying to make a sucker out of somebody?"

Personally, I always claim that Joey Perhaps has a right to reject the red feather, because for all I know he may prefer a blue feather, which means the Yales, but what I say is he does not need to be so impolite to an old guy such as Mr. Phillips Randolph, although of course Joey has no way of knowing at this time about Mr. Phillips Randolph having so much dough.

Anyway, Mr. Phillips Randolph stands staring at Joey as if he is greatly startled, and the chances are he is, at that, for the chances are nobody ever speaks to him in such a manner in all his life, and Joey Perhaps also stands there a minute staring back at Mr. Phillips Randolph, and finally Joey speaks as follows:

"Take a good peek," Joey Perhaps says. "Maybe you will remember me if you ever see me again."

"Yes," Mr. Phillips Randolph says, very quiet. "Maybe I will. They say I have a good memory for faces. I beg your pardon for stopping you, sir. It is all in fun, but I am sorry," he says.

Then Joey Perhaps goes on, and he does not seem to notice Meyer Marmalade and me sitting there in the car, and Mr. Phillips Randolph sits down, and his face is redder than somewhat, and all the joy is gone out of him, and out of his party, too. Personally, I am very sorry Joey Perhaps comes along, because I figure Mr. Phillips Randolph will give me one of his spare feathers, and I will consider it a wonderful keepsake.

But now there is not much more talking, and no laughing whatever in Mr. Phillips Randolph's party, and he just sits there as if he is thinking, and for all I know he may be thinking that there ought to be a law against a guy speaking so disrespectfully to a guy with all his dough as Joey Perhaps speaks to him.

Well, the contest of skill and science between Lefty Ledoux and Mickey McCoy turns out to be something of a disappointment, and, in fact, it is a stinkeroo, because there is little skill and no science whatever in it, and by the fourth round the customers are scuffing their feet, and saying throw these bums out, and making other derogatory remarks, and furthermore it seems that this Koons does not have either one of the judges, or even as much as the referee, in the satchel, and Ledoux gets the duke by unanimous vote of the officials.

So Meyer Marmalade is out a couple of C's, which is all he can wager at the ringside, because it seems that nobody in Boston, Mass., cares a cuss about who wins the contest, and Meyer is much disgusted with life, and so am I, and we go back to the Copley Plaza Hotel, where we are stopping, and sit down in the lobby to meditate on the injustice of everything.

Well, the lobby is a scene of gaiety, as it seems there are a number of football dinners and dances going on in the hotel, and guys and dolls in evening clothes are all around and about, and the dolls are so young and beautiful that I get to thinking that this is not such a bad old world, after all, and even Meyer Marmalade begins taking notice.

All of a sudden, a very, very beautiful young doll who is about forty percent in and sixty percent out of an evening gown walks right up to us sitting there, and holds out her hand to me, and speaks as follows:

"Do you remember me?"

Naturally, I do not remember her, but naturally I am not going to admit it, because it is never my policy to discourage any doll who wishes to strike up an acquaintance with me, which is what I figure this doll is trying to do; then I see that she is nobody but Doria Logan, one of the prettiest dolls that ever hits Broadway, and about the same time Meyer Marmalade also recognizes her.

Doria changes no little since last I see her, which is quite some time back, but there is no doubt the change is for the better, because she is once a very rattle-headed young doll, and now she seems older, and quieter, and even prettier than ever. Naturally, Meyer Marmalade and I are glad to see her looking so well, and we ask her how are tricks, and what is the good word, and all this and that, and finally Doria Logan states to us as follows:

"I am in great trouble," Doria says. "I am in terrible trouble, and you are the first ones I see that I can talk to about it."

Well, at this, Meyer Marmalade begins to tuck in somewhat, because he figures it is the old lug coming up, and Meyer Marmalade is not such a guy as will go for the lug from a doll unless he gets something more than a story. But I can see Doria Logan is in great earnest.

"Do you remember Joey Perhaps?" she says.

"A wrong gee," Meyer Marmalade says. "A dead wrong gee."

"I not only remember Joey Perhaps," I say, "but I see him on the train today."

"Yes," Doria says, "he is here in town. He hunts me up only a few hours ago. He is here to do me great harm. He is here to finish ruining my life."

"A wrong gee," Meyer Marmalade puts in again. "Always a hundred percent wrong gee."

Then Doria Logan gets us to go with her to a quiet corner of the lobby, and she tells us a strange story, as follows, and also to wit:

It seems that she is once tangled up with Joey Perhaps, which is something I never know before, and neither does Meyer Marmalade, and, in fact, the news shocks us quite some. It is back in the days when she is just about sixteen and is in the chorus of Earl Carroll's Vanities, and I remember well what a standout she is for looks, to be sure.

Naturally, at sixteen, Doria is quite a chump doll, and does not know which way is south, or what time it is, which is the way all dolls at sixteen are bound to be, and she has no idea what a wrong gee Joey Perhaps is, as he is good-looking, and young, and seems very romantic, and is always speaking of love and one thing and another.

Well, the upshot of it all is the upshot of thousands of other cases since chump dolls commence coming to Broadway, and the first thing she knows, Doria Logan finds herself mixed up with a very bad character, and does not know what to do about it.

By and by, Joey Perhaps commences mistreating her no little, and finally he tries to use her in some nefarious schemes of his, and of course everybody along Broadway knows that most of Joey's schemes are especially nefarious, because Joey is on the shake almost since infancy.

Well, one day Doria says to herself that if this is love, she has all she can stand, and she hauls off and runs away from Joey Perhaps. She goes back to her people, who live in the city of Cambridge, Mass., which is the same place where the Harvards have their college, and she goes there because she does not know of any other place to go.

It seems that Doria's people are poor, and Doria goes to a

business school and learns to be a stenographer, and she is working for a guy in the real estate dodge by the name of Poopnoodle, and doing all right for herself, and in the meantime she hears that Joey Perhaps gets sent away, so she figures her troubles are all over as far as he is concerned.

Now Doria Logan goes along quietly through life, working for Mr. Poopnoodle, and never thinking of love, or anything of a similar nature, when she meets up with a young guy who is one of the Harvards, and who is maybe twenty-one years old, and is quite a football player, and where Doria meets up with this guy is in a drug store over a banana split.

Well, the young Harvard takes quite a fancy to Doria and, in fact, he is practically on fire about her, but by this time Doria is going on twenty, and is no longer a chump doll, and she has no wish to get tangled up in love again.

In fact, whenever she thinks of Joey Perhaps, Doria takes to hating guys in general, but somehow she cannot seem to get up a real good hate on the young Harvard, because, to hear her tell it, he is handsome, and noble, and has wonderful ideals.

Now as time goes on, Doria finds she is growing pale, and is losing her appetite, and cannot sleep, and this worries her no little, as she is always a first-class feeder, and finally she comes to the conclusion that what ails her is that she is in love with the young Harvard, and can scarcely live without him, so she admits as much to him one night when the moon is shining on the Charles River, and everything is a dead cold setup for love.

Well, naturally, after a little offhand guzzling, which is quite permissible under the circumstances, the young guy wishes her to name the happy day, and Doria has half a notion to make it the following Monday, this being a Sunday night, but then she gets to thinking about her past with Joey Perhaps, and all, and she figures it will be bilking the young Harvard to marry him unless she has a small talk with him first about Joey, because she is well aware that many young guys may have some objection to wedding a doll with a skeleton in her closet, and especially a skeleton such as Joey Perhaps.

But she is so happy she does not wish to run the chance of spoiling everything by these narrations right away, so she keeps her trap closed about Joey, although she promises to marry the young Harvard when he gets out of college, which will be the following year, if he still insists, because Doria figures that by then she will be able to break the news to him about Joey very gradually, and gently, and especially gently.

Anyway, Doria says she is bound and determined to tell him before the wedding, even if he takes the wind on her as a consequence, and personally I claim this is very considerate of Doria, because many dolls never tell before the wedding, or even after. So Doria and the young Harvard are engaged, and great happiness prevails, when, all of a sudden, in pops Joey Perhaps.

It seems that Joey learns of Doria's engagement as soon as he gets out of the state institution, and he hastens to Boston, Mass., with an inside coat pocket packed with letters that Doria writes him long ago, and also a lot of pictures they have taken together, as young guys and dolls are bound to do, and while there is nothing much out of line about these letters and pictures, put them all together they spell a terrible pain in the neck to Doria at this particular time.

"A wrong gee," Meyer Marmalade says. "But," he says, "he is only going back to his old shake-down dodge, so all you have to do is to buy him off."

Well, at this, Doria Logan laughs one of these little short dry laughs that go "hah," and says like this:

"Of course he is looking to get bought off, but," she says, "where will I get any money to buy him off? I do not have a dime of my own, and Joey is talking large figures, because he knows my fiancé's papa has plenty. He wishes me to go

to my fiancé and make him get the money off his papa, or
he threatens to personally deliver the letters and pictures
to my fiancé's papa.

"You can see the predicament I am in," Doria says, "and
you can see what my fiancé's papa will think of me if he
learns I am once mixed up with a blackmailer such as Joey
Perhaps.

"Besides," Doria says, "it is something besides money
with Joey Perhaps, and I am not so sure he will not double-
cross me even if I can pay him his price. Joey Perhaps is
very angry at me. I think," she says, "if he can spoil my
happiness, it will mean more to him than money."

Well, Doria states that all she can think of when she is
talking to Joey Perhaps is to stall for time, and she tells Joey
that, no matter what, she cannot see her fiancé until after
the large football game between the Harvards and the
Yales as he has to do a little football playing for the Harvards, and Joey asks her if she is going to see the game, and
naturally she is.

And then Joey says he thinks he will look up a ticket
speculator, and buy a ticket and attend the game himself,
as he is very fond of football, and where will she be sitting,
as he hopes and trusts he will be able to see something of
her during the game, and this statement alarms Doria
Logan no little, for who is she going with but her fiancé's
papa, and a party of his friends, and she feels that there is
no telling what Joey Perhaps may be up to.

She explains to Joey that she does not know exactly
where she will be sitting, except that it will be on the
Harvards' side of the field, but Joey is anxious for more
details than this.

"In fact," Doria says, "he is most insistent, and he stands
at my elbow while I call up Mr. Randolph at this very hotel,
and he tells me the exact locations of our seats. Then Joey
says he will endeavor to get a seat as close to me as possible,
and he goes away."

"What Mr. Randolph?" Meyer says. "Which Mr. Randolph?" he says. "You do not mean Mr. Phillips Randolph, by any chance, do you?"

"Why, to be sure," Doria says. "Do you know him?"

Naturally, from now on Meyer Marmalade gazes at Doria Logan with deep respect, and so do I, although by now she is crying a little, and I am by no means in favor of crying dolls. But while she is crying, Meyer Marmalade seems to be doing some more thinking, and finally he speaks as follows:

"Kindly see if you can recall these locations you speak of."

So here is where the football game comes in once more.

Only I regret to state that personally I do not witness this game, and the reason I do not witness it is because nobody wakes me up the next day in time for me to witness it, and the way I look at it, this is all for the best, as I am scarcely a football enthusiast.

So from now on the story belongs to Meyer Marmalade, and I will tell you as Meyer tells it to me.

It is a most exciting game (Meyer says). The place is full of people, and there are bands playing, and much cheering, and more lovely dolls than you can shake a stick at, although I do not believe there are any lovelier present than Doria Logan.

It is a good thing she remembers the seat locations, otherwise I will never find her, but there she is surrounded by some very nice-looking people, including Mr. Phillips Randolph, and there I am two rows back of Mr. Phillips Randolph, and the ticket spec I get my seat off of says he cannot understand why everybody wishes to sit near Mr. Phillips Randolph today when there are other seats just as good, and maybe better, on the Harvards' side.

So I judge he has other calls similar to mine for this location, and a sweet price he gets for it, too, and I judge that maybe at least one call is from Joey Perhaps, as I see Joey a couple of rows on back up where I am sitting, but off to my left on an aisle, while I am almost in a direct line with Mr. Phillips Randolph.

To show you that Joey is such a guy as attracts attention, Mr. Phillips Randolph stands up a few minutes before the game starts, peering around and about to see who is present that he knows, and all of a sudden his eyes fall on Joey Perhaps, and then Mr. Phillips Randolph proves he has a good memory for faces, to be sure, for he states as follows:

"Why," he says, "there is the chap who rebuffs me so churlishly on the train when I offer him our colors. Yes," he says, "I am sure it is the same chap."

Well, what happens in the football game is much pulling and hauling this way and that, and to and fro, between the Harvards and the Yales without a tally right down to the last five minutes of play, and then all of a sudden the Yales shove the football down to within about three-eights of an inch of the Harvards' goal line.

At this moment quite some excitement prevails. Then the next thing anybody knows, the Yales outshove the Harvards, and now the game is over, and Mr. Phillips Randolph gets up out of his seat, and I hear Mr. Phillips Randolph say like this:

"Well," he says, "the score is not so bad as it might be, and it is a wonderful game, and," he says, "we seem to make one convert to our cause, anyway, for see who is wearing our colors."

And with this he points to Joey Perhaps, who is still sitting down, with people stepping around him and over him, and he is still smiling a little smile, and Mr. Phillips Randolph seems greatly pleased to see that Joey Perhaps has a big, broad crimson ribbon where he once wears his white silk muffler.

But the chances are Mr. Phillips Randolph will be greatly surprised if he knows that the crimson ribbon across Joey's bosom comes of Ollie Ortega planting a short knife in Joey's throat, or do I forget to mention before that Ollie Ortega is among those present?

I send for Ollie after I leave you last night, figuring he may love to see a nice football game. He arrives by plane this morning, and I am not wrong in my figuring. Ollie thinks the game is swell.

Well, personally, I will never forget this game, it is so exciting. Just after the tally comes off, all of a sudden, from the Yales in the stand across the field from the Harvards, comes a long, drawn-out wail that sounds so mournful it makes me feel very sad, to be sure. It starts off something like Oh-oh-oh-oh-oh, with all the Yales Oh-oh-oh-oh-oh-ing at once, and I ask a guy next to me what it is all about.

"Why," the guy says, "it is the Yales' 'Undertaker Song.' They always sing it when they have the other guy licked. I am an old Yale myself, and I will now personally sing this song for you."

And with this the guy throws back his head, and opens his mouth wide and lets out a yowl like a wolf calling to its mate.

Well, I stop the guy, and tell him it is a very lovely song, to be sure, and quite appropriate all the way around, and then I hasten away from the football game without getting a chance to say good-by to Doria, although afterwards I mail her the package of letters and pictures that Ollie gets out of Joey Perhaps' inside coat pocket during the confusion that prevails when the Yales make their tally, and I hope and trust that she will think the crimson streaks across the package are just a little touch of color in honor of the Harvards.

But the greatest thing about the football game (Meyer Marmalade says) is I win two C's off of one of the Harvards sitting near me, so I am now practically even on my trip.

The Idol of the Flies

§ BY JANE RICE

PRUITT watched a fly on the corner of the table. He held himself very still. The fly cleaned its wings with short, backstroke motions of its legs. It looked, Pruitt thought, like Crippled Harry. He hated him almost as much as he hated Aunt Mona. But he hated Miss Bittner most of all.

He lifted his head and bared his teeth at the nape of Miss Bittner's neck. He hated the way she stood there erasing the blackboard in great, sweeping circles. He hated the way her shoulderblades poked out. He hated the big horn comb thrust into her thin hair—thrust not quite far enough —so that some of the hair flapped. And he hated the way she arranged it around her sallow face and low on her neck, to conceal the little button that nestled in one large-lobed ear. The button and the narrow black cord that ran down the back of her dress under her starched collar.

He liked the button and the cord. He liked them because Miss Bittner hated them. She pretended she didn't care about being deaf. But she did. And she pretended she liked him. But she didn't.

He made her nervous. It was easy. All he had to do was open his eyes wide and stare at her without batting. It was delightfully simple. Too simple. It wasn't fun any more. He was glad he had found out about the flies.

Miss Bittner placed the eraser precisely in the center of the blackboard runnel, dusted her hands and turned toward Pruitt. Pruitt opened his eyes quite wide and gimleted her with an unblinking stare.

Miss Bittner cleared her throat nervously. "That will be all, Pruitt. Tomorrow we will begin on derivatives."

"Yes, Miss Bittner," Pruitt said loudly, meticulously forming the words with his lips.

Miss Bittner flushed. She straightened the collar of her dress.

"Your aunt said you might take a swim."

"Yes, Miss Bittner."

"Good afternoon, Pruitt. Tea at five."

"Yes, Miss Bittner. Good afternoon, Miss Bittner." Pruitt lowered his gaze to a point three inches below Miss Bittner's knees. He allowed a faint expression of controlled surprise to wrinkle his forehead.

Involuntarily, Miss Bittner glanced down. Quick as a flash, Pruitt swept his hand across the table and scooped up the fly. When Miss Bittner again raised her head, Pruitt was regarding her blandly. He arose.

"There's some lemonade on top of the back-porch icebox. Can I have some?"

"May I have some, Pruitt."

"May I have some?"

"Yes, Pruitt, you may."

Pruitt crossed the room to the door.

"Pruitt—"

Pruitt stopped, swiveled slowly on his heel and stared unwinkingly at his tutor. "Yes, Miss Bittner?"

"Let's remember not to slam the screen door, shall we? It disturbs your auntie, you know." Miss Bittner twitched her pale lips into what she mistakenly believed was the smile of a friendly conspirator.

Pruitt gazed at her steadily. "Yes, Miss Bittner."

"That's fine," said Clara Bittner with false heartiness.

"Is that all, Miss Bittner?"

"Yes, Pruitt."

Pruitt, without relaxing his basilisk-like contemplation of his unfortunate tutor, counted up to twelve, then he turned and quitted the room.

Clara Bittner looked at the empty doorway a long while and then she shuddered. Had she been pressed for an explanation of that shudder she couldn't have given a satisfactory answer. In all probability, she would have said, with a vague conciliatory gesture, "I don't know. I think, perhaps, it's a bit difficult for a child to warm up to a teacher." And, no doubt, she would have added brightly, "The psychology of the thing, you know."

Miss Bittner was a stanch defender of psychology. She had taken a summer course in it—ten years ago—and had, as she was fond of repeating, received the highest grades in the class. It never occurred to Miss Bittner that this was due to her aptitude at memorizing whole paragraphs and being able to transpose these onto her test papers without ever having digested the kernels of thought contained therein.

Miss Bittner stooped and unlaced one oxford. She breathed a sigh of relief. She sat erect, pulled down her dress in back and then felt with her fingertips the rubbery black cord dangling against her neck. Miss Bittner sighed again. A buzzing at one of the windows claimed her attention.

She went to a cupboard which yielded up a wire fly swatter. Grasping this militantly, she strode to the window, drew back, closed her eyes, and swatted. The fly, badly battered, dropped to the sill, lay on its wings, its legs curled.

She unhooked the screen and with the end of the swatter delicately urged the corpse outside.

"Ugh," said Miss Bittner. And had Miss Bittner been pressed for an explanation of that *ugh* she, likewise, would have been at a loss for a satisfactory answer. It was strange how she felt about flies. They affected her much as rattle-snakes would have. It wasn't that they were germy, or that their eyes were a reddish orange and, so she had heard, reflected everything in the manner of prisms; it wasn't that they had the odious custom of regurgitating a drop of their last meal before beginning on a new one; it wasn't the crooked hairy legs, nor the probing proboscis; it was—well, it was just the creatures themselves. Possibly, Miss Bittner might have said, simpering to show that she really didn't mean it, "I have flyophobia."

The truth was, she did. She was afraid of them. Deathly afraid. As some people are afraid of enclosed areas, as others are afraid of height, so Miss Bittner was afraid of flies. Childishly, senselessly, but horribly, afraid.

She returned the swatter to the cupboard and forthwith scrubbed her hands thoroughly at the sink. It was odd, she thought, how many flies she had encountered lately. It almost seemed as if someone were purposely diverting a channel of flies her way. She smiled to herself at this fool-ish whimsy, wiped her hands and tidied her hair. Now for some of that lemonade. She was pleased that Pruitt had mentioned it. If he hadn't, she might not have known it was there and she did so love lemonade.

Pruitt stood at the head of the stairwell. He worked his jaws convulsively, then he pursed his mouth, leaned far over the polished banister and spat. The globule of spittle elongated into a pear-shaped tear and flattened with a wet smack on the floor below.

Pruitt went on down the stairs. He could feel the fly bumbling angrily in its hot, moist prison. He put his tightly curled hand to his lips and blew into the tunnel made by his thumb and forefinger. The fly clung for dear life to his creased palm.

At the foot of the stairs Pruitt paused long enough to squeeze each one of the tiny green balls on the ends of the fern that was potted in an intricate and artistic copper holder.

Then he went through a hallway into the kitchen.

"Give me a glass," he said to the ample-bosomed woman who sat on a stool, picking nut meats and putting them into a glass bowl.

The woman heaved herself to her feet.

" 'Please' won't hurt you," the woman said.

"I don't have to say 'please' to you. You're the help."

The cook put her hands on her hips. "What you need is a thrashing," she said grimly. "A good, sound thrashing."

By way of reply, Pruitt snatched the paper sack of cracked hulls and deliberately up-ended the bag into the bowl of nut meats.

The woman made a futile grab. Her heavy face grew suffused with a wave of rich color. She opened her hand and brought it up in a swinging arc.

Pruitt planted his feet firmly on the linoleum and said low, "I'll scream. You know what that'll do to Aunt."

The woman held her hand poised so for a second and then let it fall to her aproned side. "You brat," she hissed; "you sneaking, pink-eyed brat!"

"Give me a glass."

The woman reached up on a shelf of the cabinet, took down a glass and wordlessly handed it to the boy.

"I don't want that one," Pruitt said, "I want that one." He pointed to the glass's identical twin on the topmost shelf.

Silently, the woman padded across the floor and pushed a short kitchen ladder over to the cabinet. Silently, she climbed it. Silently, she handed down the designated glass.

Pruitt accepted it. "I'm going to tell Aunt Mona you took your shoes off."

The woman climbed down the ladder, put it away and returned to the bowl.

"Harry is a dirty you-know-what," Pruitt said.

The woman went on lifting out the nut hulls.

"He stinks."

The woman went on lifting out the nut hulls.

"So do you," finished Pruitt. He waited.

The woman went on lifting out the nut hulls.

The boy took his glass and repaired to the back porch. It spoiled the fun when they didn't talk back. Cook was on to him. But she wouldn't complain. Aunt Mona let them stay through the winter rent free with nobody but themselves to see to and Harry was a cripple and couldn't make a living. She wouldn't dast complain.

Pruitt lifted the pitcher of lemonade from the lid of the icebox and poured himself a glassful. He drank half of it and let the rest dribble along a crack, holding the glass close to the floor so it wouldn't make a trickling noise. When it dried it would be sweet and sticky. Lots of flies.

He relaxed his hand ever so slightly and dexterously extricated his shopworn captive. It hummed furiously. Pruitt pulled off one of its wings and dropped the mutilated insect into the lemonade. It kicked ineffectually, was quiet, kicked again, and was quiet—drifting on the surface of the liquid, sagging to one side, its remaining wing outstretched like a useless sail.

The boy caught it and pushed it under. "I christen you Miss Bittner," he said. He released his hold and the fly popped to the top—a piece of lemon pulp on its back. It kicked again—feebly—and was quiet.

Pruitt replaced the lemonade and opened the screen door. He pulled it so that the spring twanged protestingly. He let go and leaped down the steps. The door came to with a mighty bang behind'him. That was the finish of Aunt Mona's nap.

He crouched on his haunches and listened. A cloud shadow floated across the grass. A butterfly teetered uncertainly on a waxy leaf, and fluttered away following an erratic air trail of its own. A June bug drummed through the warm afternoon, its armored belly a shiny bottle-green streak in the sunlight. Pruitt crumbled the cone of an ant hill and watched the excited maneuvers of its inhabitants.

There was the slow drag of footsteps somewhere above— the opening of a shutter. Pruitt grinned. His ears went up and back with the broadness of it. Cook would puff up two

flights of stairs "out of the goodness of her heart," Aunt
Mona said—"out of dumbness," if you asked him. Whyn't
she let "Miss Mona" fill her own bloody icebag? There'd be
time to go in and mix the nut shells up again. But no, he
might run into Miss Bittner beating a thirsty course to the
lemonade. She might guess about the fly. Besides, he'd
dallied too long as it was. He had business to attend to.
Serious business.

He got up, stretched, scrunched his heel on the ant hill
and walked away in the direction of the bathhouse.

Twice he halted to shy stones at a plump robin and once
he froze into a statue as there was a movement in the path
before him. His quick eyes fastened on a toad squatted in
the dust, its bulgy sides going in and out, in and out, like a
miniature bellows. Stealthily, Pruitt broke off a twig. In
and out, in and out, in and out. Pruitt eased forward. In and
out, in and out, in and out. He could see its toes spread far
apart, the dappling of spots on its cool, froggy skin. In and
out, in and out, the leg muscles tensed as the toad prepared
to make another hop. Pantherlike, Pruitt leaped, his hand
descending. The toad emitted an agonized, squeaking
scream.

Pruitt stood up and looked at the toad with amusement.
The twig protruded from its sloping back. In and out, in
and out went the toad's sides. In—and out, in—and out. It
essayed an unstable hop, leaving a darkish stain in its
wake. Again it hopped. The twig remained stanchly upright. The third hop was shorter. Barely its own length.
Pruitt nosed it over into the grass with his shoe. In—and—
out went the toad's sides, in—and—out, in—and—out, in—

Pruitt walked on.

The crippled man mending his fishing net on the wooden
pier sensed his approaching footsteps. With as much haste
as his wracked spine would permit, the man got to his feet.
Pruitt heard the scrambling and quickened his pace.

"Hello," he said innocently.

The man bobbed his head. "Do, Mr. Pruitt."

"Mending your nets?"

"Yes, Mr. Pruitt."

"I guess the dock is a good place to do it."

"Yes, Mr. Pruitt." The man licked his tongue across his lips and his eyes made rapid sorties to the right and left, as if seeking a means of escape.

Pruitt scraped his shoe across the wooden planking. "Excepting that it gets fish scales all over everything," he said softly, "and I don't like fish scales."

The man's Adam's apple jerked up and down as he swallowed thrice in rapid succession. He wiped his hands on his pants.

"I said I don't like fish scales."

"Yes, Mr. Pruitt, I didn't mean to—"

"So I guess maybe I better fix it so there won't be any fish scales any more."

"Mr. Pruitt, please, I didn't—" His voice petered out as the boy picked up a corner of the net.

"Not ever any more fish scales," said Pruitt.

"Don't pull it," the man begged, "it'll snag on the dock."

"I won't snag it," Pruitt said: "I wouldn't snag it for anything." He smiled at Harry. "Because if I just snagged it, you'd just mend it again and then there'd be more fish scales, and I don't like fish scales." Bunching the net in his fists, he dragged it to the edge of the dock. "So I'll just throw it in the water and then I guess there won't ever be any more fish scales."

Harry's jaw went slack with shocked disbelief. "Mr. Pruitt—" he began.

"Like this," said Pruitt. He held the net out at arm's length over the pier and relinquished his clasp.

With an inarticulate cry the man threw himself awkwardly on the planking in a vain attempt to retrieve his slowly vanishing property.

"Now there won't ever be any more fish scales," Pruitt said. "Not ever any more."

Harry hefted himself to his knees. His face was white. For one dull, weighted minute he looked at his tormentor. Then he struggled to his feet and limped away without a word.

Pruitt considered his deformed posture with the eye of a connoisseur. "Harry is a hunchback," he sang after him in a lilting childish treble. "Harry is a hunchback, Harry is a hunchback."

The man limped on, one shoulder dipping sharply with each successive step, his coarse shirt stretched over his misshapen back. A bend in the path hid him from view.

Pruitt pushed open the door of the bathhouse and went inside. He closed the door behind him and bolted it. He waited until his eyes had become accustomed to the semi-gloom, whereupon he went over to a cot against the wall, lifted up its faded chintz spread, felt underneath and pulled out two boxes. He sat down and delved into their contents.

From the first he produced a section of a bread board, four pegs, and six half-burned birthday candles screwed into nibbled-looking pink candy rosettes. The bread board he placed on top the pegs, the candles he arranged in a semicircle. He surveyed the result with squint-eyed approval.

From the second box he removed a grotesque object composed of coal tar. It perched shakily on pipestem legs, two strips of cellophane were pasted to its flanks, and a black rubber band dangled downward from its head in which was embedded—one on each side—red cinnamon drops.

The casual observer would have seen in this sculpture a child's crude efforts to emulate the characteristics of the common housefly. The casual observer—if he had been inclined to go on with his observing—also would have seen that Pruitt was in a "mood." He might even have observed aloud, "That child looks positively feverish and he shouldn't be allowed to play with matches."

But at the moment there was no casual observer. Only

Pruitt absorbed in lighting the birthday candles. The image of the fly he deposited square in the middle of the bread board.

Cross-legged he sat, chin down, arms folded. He rocked himself back and forth. He began to chant. Singsong. Through his nose. Once in a while he rolled his eyes around in their sockets, but merely once in a while. He had found, if he did that too often, it made him dizzy.

"O Idol of the Flies," intoned Pruitt, "hahneemahneemo." He scratched his ankle ruminatively. "Hahneeweemahneemo," he improved, "make the lemonade dry in the crack on the back porch, and make Miss Bittner find the scrooched-up fly after she's already drunk some, and make cook go down in the cellar for some marmalade and make her not turn on the light and make her fall over the string I've got tied between the posts, and make Aunt get a piece of nutshell in her bread and cough like hell." Pruitt thought this over. "Hell," he said, "hell, hell, hell, hell, HELL."

He meditated in silence. "I guess that's all," he said finally, "except maybe you'd better fill up my fly catcher in case we have currant cookies for tea. Hahneeweemahneemo, O Idol of the Flies, you are free to GO!"

Pruitt fixed his gaze in the middle distance and riveted it there. Motionless, scarcely breathing, his lips parted, he huddled on the bare boards—a small sphinx in khaki shorts.

This was what Pruitt called "not-thinking-time." Pretty soon, entirely without volition on his part, queer, half-formed dream things would float through his mind. Like dark polliwogs. Propelling themselves along with their tails, hinting at secrets that nobody knew, not even grown-ups. Some day he would be able to catch one, quickly, before it wriggled off into the inner hidden chamber where They had a nest and then he would know. He would catch it in a net of thought, like Harry's net caught fishes, and no matter how it squirmed and threshed about he would pin it flat against his skull until he knew. Once, he had almost caught one. He had been on the very rim of knowing and Miss Bittner had come down to bring him some peanut butter sandwiches and it had escaped back into that deep, strange place in his mind where They lived. He had only had it for a split second but he remembered it had blind, weepy eyes and was smooth.

If Miss Bittner hadn't come— He had vomited on her stockings. Here came one of Them now—fast, it was coming fast, too fast to catch. It was gone, leaving behind it a heady exhilaration. Here came another, revolving, writhing like a sea snake, indistinct, shadowy. Let it go, the next one might be lured into the net. Here it came, two of them, roiling in the sleep hollows. Easily now, easily, easily, close in, easily, so there wouldn't be any warning ripples, closer, they weren't watching, murmuring to each other—there! He had them!

"Pruitt. Oh, Pruitt."

The things veered away, their tails whipping his intellect into a spinning mass of chaotic frenzy.

"Pru—itt. Where are you? Pru—itt."

The boy blinked.

"Pru—itt. Oh, Pru—itt."

His mouth distorted like that of an enraged animal. He stuck out his tongue and hissed at the locked door. The handle turned.

"Pruitt, are you in there?"

"Yes, Miss Bittner." The words were thick and meaty in his mouth. If he bit down, Pruitt thought, he could bite one in two and chew it up and it would squish out between his teeth like an eclair.

"Unlock the door."

"Yes, Miss Bittner."

Pruitt blew out the candles and swept his treasures under the cot. He reconsidered this action, shoved his hand under the chintz skirt, snaffled the coal-tar fly and stuffed it into his shirt.

"Do you hear me, Pruitt? Unlock this door." The knob rattled.

"I'm coming fast as I can," he said. He rose, stalked over to the door, shot back the bolt and stood, squinting, in the brilliant daylight before Miss Bittner.

"What on earth are you doing in there?"

"I guess I must've fallen asleep."

Miss Bittner peered into the murky confines of the bathhouse. She sniffed inquisitively.

"Pruitt," she said, "have you been smoking?"

"No, Miss Bittner."

"We mustn't tell a falsehood, Pruitt. It is far better to tell the truth and accept the consequences."

"I haven't been smoking." Pruitt could feel his stomach moving inside him. He was going to be sick again. Like he was the last time. Miss Bittner was wavering in front of him. Her outside edges were all blurry. His stomach gave a violent lurch. Pruitt looked at Miss Bittner's stockings. They were messy. Awfully messy. Miss Bittner looked at them, too.

"Run along up to the house, Pruitt," she said kindly. "I'll be up presently."

"Yes, Miss Bittner."

"And we won't say anything about smoking to your auntie. I think you've been sufficiently punished."

"Yes, Miss Bittner."

"Run along, now."

Pruitt went languidly up the path, conscious of Miss Bittner's eyes boring into him. When he turned the bend, he stopped and crept slyly into the bushes. He made his way back toward the bathhouse, pressing the branches away from him and easing them cautiously to prevent them from snapping.

Miss Bittner sat on the steps taking off her stockings. She rinsed her legs in the water and dried them with her handkerchief. Pruitt could see an oval corn plaster on her little toe. She put her bony feet into her patent-leather Health

Eases, got up, brushed her dress and disappeared into the bathhouse.

Pruitt inched nearer.

Miss Bittner came to the doorway and examined something she held in her hands. She looked puzzled. From his vantage point, Pruitt glimpsed the pink of the candy rosettes, the stubby candle wicks.

"I hate you," Pruitt whispered venomously, "I hate you, I hate you." Tenderly he withdrew the coal-tar image from his shirt. He cuddled it against his cheek. "Break her ear thing," he muttered. "Break it all to pieces so's she'll have to act deaf. Break it, break it, hahneeweemahneemo, break it good." Warily he crawled backward until he regained the path.

He trudged onward, pausing only twice. Once at a break in the hedge where he reached into the aperture and drew forth a cone-shaped contraption smeared with syrup. Five flies clung to this, their wings sticky, their legs gluey. These he disengaged, ignoring the lesser fry of gnats and midges that had met a similar fate, and returned the flycatcher to its lair. The second interruption along his line of march was a sort of interlude during which he cracked the two-inch spine of a garden lizard and hung it on a bramble where it performed incredibly tortuous convolutions with the lower half of its body.

Mona Eagleston came out of her bedroom and closed the door gently behind her. Everything about Mona was gentle from the top of her wren-brown head threaded with gray to the slippers on her ridiculously tiny feet. She was rather like a fawn. An aging fawn with liquid eyes that, despite the encroaching years, had failed to lose their tiptoe look of expectancy.

One knew instinctively that Mona Eagleston was that rare phenomenon—a lady to the manor born. If, occasionally, when in close proximity with her nephew, a perplexed look overshadowed that delicate face, it was no more than a passing cloud. Children were inherently good. If they appeared otherwise, it was simply because their actions were misunderstood. They—he—Pruitt didn't mean to do things. He couldn't know that—well, that slamming the screen door, for instance, could send a sickening stab of pain through a head racked with migraine. He couldn't be expected to know, the poor orphan lamb. The poor, dear, orphan lamb.

If only she didn't have to pour at teatime. If only she could lie quiet and still with a cold compress on her head and the shutters pulled to. How selfish she was. Teatimes to a child were lovely, restful periods. Moments to be forever cherished in the pattern of memory. Like colorful loops of embroidery floss embellishing the whole. A skein of golden, shining teatimes with the sunset staining the windows and highlighting the fat-sided delft milk jug. The taste of jam, the brown crumbs left on the cookie plate, the teacups—eggshell frail—with handles like wedding rings. All of these were precious to a child. Deep down inside, without quite knowing why, they absorbed such things as sponges absorbed water—and, like sponges, they could wring these memories out when they were growing old. As she did, sometimes. What a wretched person she was to begrudge a teatime to Pruitt, dear little Pruitt, her own dead brother's child.

She went on down the stairs, one white hand trailing the banister. The fern, she noticed, was dying. This was the third fern. She'd always had so much luck with ferns, until lately. Her goldfish, too. They had died. It was almost an omen. And Pruitt's turtles. She had bought them at the village. So cunning they were with enameled pictures on their hard, tree-barky shells. They had died. She mustn't think about dying. The doctor had said it was bad for her.

She crossed the great hall and entered the drawing room.

"Dear Pruitt," she said to the boy swinging his legs from the edge of a brocaded chair. She kissed him. She had intended to kiss his sunwarm cheek but he had moved, suddenly, and the kiss had met an unresponsive ear. Children were jumpy little things.

"Did you have a nice day?"

"Yes, Aunt."

"And you, Miss Bittner? Did you have a nice day? And how did the conjugations go this morning? Did our young man . . . why, my dear, whatever is the matter?"

"She broke her ear thing," Pruitt said. He turned toward his tutor and enunciated in an exaggerated fashion, "Didn't you, Miss Bittner?"

Miss Bittner reddened. She spoke in the unnaturally loud, toneless voice of the deaf. "I dropped my hearing aid," she explained. "On the bathroom floor. I'm afraid, until I get it fixed, that you'll have to bear with me." She smiled a tight strained smile to show that it was really quite a joke on her.

"What a shame," said Mona Eagleston. "But I daresay it can be repaired in the village. Harry can take it in tomorrow."

Miss Bittner followed the movement of Mona Eagleston's lips almost desperately.

"No," she said hesitantly, "Harry didn't do it. I did it. The bathroom tile, you know. It was frightfully clumsy of me."

"And she drank some lemonade that had a fly in it. Didn't you, Miss Bittner? I said you drank some lemonade that had a fly in it, didn't you?"

Miss Bittner nodded politely. Her eyes focused on Pruitt's mouth.

"Cry?" she ventured. "No, I didn't cry."

Mona Eagleston seated herself behind the tea caddy and prepared to pour. She must warn cook hereafter to put an oiled cover over the lemonade. One couldn't be too particular where children were concerned. They were susceptible to all sorts of diseases and flies were notorious carriers. If Pruitt were taken ill because of her lack of forethought, she would never forgive herself. Never.

"Could I have some marmalade?" Pruitt asked.

"We have currant cookies, dear, and nut bread. Do you think we need marmalade?"

"I do so love marmalade, Aunt. Miss Bittner does too. Don't you, Miss Bittner?"

Miss Bittner smiled stoically on and accepted her cup with a pleasant noncommittal murmur that she devoutly hoped would serve as an appropriate answer to whatever Pruitt was asking.

"Very well, dear." Mona tinkled a bell.

"I'll pass the cookies, Aunt."

"Thank you, Pruitt. You are very thoughtful."

The boy took the plate and carried it over to Miss Bittner and an expression of acute suffering swam across the Bittner countenance as the boy trod heavily on her foot.

"Have some cookies." Pruitt thrust the plate at her.

"That's quite all right," Miss Bittner said, thinking he had apologized and congratulating herself on the fact that she hadn't moaned aloud. If he had known she had a corn, he couldn't have selected the location with more exactitude. She looked at the cookies. After that lemonade episode, she had felt she couldn't eat again—but they were tempting. Gracious, how that corn ached.

"Here's a nice curranty one." Pruitt popped a cookie on her plate.

"Thank you, Pruitt."

Cook waddled into the room. "Did you ring, Miss Mona?"

"Yes, Bertha. Would you get Pruitt some marmalade, please?"

Bertha shot a poisonous glance at Pruitt. "There's none up, ma'am. Will the jam do?"

Pruitt managed a sorrowful sigh. "I do so love marmalade, Aunt," and then happily, as if it were an afterthought, "Isn't there some in the basement cubby?"

Mona Eagleston made a helpless moue at cook. "Would you mind terribly, Bertha? You know how children are."

"Yes, ma'am, I know how children are," cook said in a flat voice.

"Thank you, Bertha. The pineapple will do."

"Yes, ma'am." Bertha plodded away.

"She was walking around in her bare feet again today," Pruitt said.

His aunt shook her head sadly. "I don't know what to do," she said to Miss Bittner. "I dislike being cross, but ever since she stepped on that nail"—Mona Eagleston smiled quickly at her nephew—"not that you meant to leave it there, darling, but . . . well . . . will you have a slice of nut bread, Miss Bittner?"

Pruitt licked back a grin. "Aunt said would you like a slice of nut bread, Miss Bittner," he repeated ringingly.

Miss Bittner paid no heed. She seemed to be in a frozen trance sitting as she did rigidly upright staring at her plate with horror. She arose.

"I . . . I don't feel well," she said. "I think . . . I think I'd better go lie down."

Pruitt hopped off his chair and took her plate. Mona Eagleston made a distressed *tch*ing sound. "Is there anything I can do—" She half rose but Miss Bittner waved her back.

"It's nothing," Miss Bittner said hoarsely. "I . . . I think it's just something I . . . I ate. Don't let me disturb your t-t-teatime." She put her napkin over her mouth and hastily hobbled from the room.

"I should see that she—" began Mona Eagleston worriedly.

"Oh, don't let's ruin teatime," Pruitt interposed hurriedly. "Here, have some nut bread. It looks dreadfully good."

"Well—"

"Please, Aunt Mona. Not teatime."

"Very well, Pruitt." Mona chose a slice of bread. "Does teatime mean a great deal to you? It did to me when I was a little girl."

"Yes, Aunt." He watched her break a morsel of bread, butter it and put it in her mouth.

"I used to live for teatime. It was such a cozy—" Mona

Eagleston lifted a pale hand to her throat. She began to cough. Her eyes filled with tears. She looked wildly around for water. She tried to say "water" but she couldn't get the word past the choking in her lungs. If Pruitt would only— but he was just a child. He couldn't be expected to know what to do for a coughing spell. Poor, dear Pruitt, he looked so . . . so perturbed. Handing her the tea like that, his face all puckery. She gulped down a great draught of the scalding liquid. Her slight frame was seized with a paroxysm of coughing. Mercy! She must have mistakenly put salt in it instead of sugar.

She wiped her brimming eyes. "Nutshell," she wheezed, gaining her feet. "Back . . . presently—" Coughing violently, she too quitted the room.

From somewhere beneath Pruitt's feet, deep in the bowels of the house, came a faint, faraway thud.

Pruitt picked the flies off Miss Bittner's cookie. Where there had been five, there were now four and a half. He put the remains in his pocket. They might come in handy.

Dimly he heard cook calling for help. It was a smothered hysterical calling. If Aunt Mona didn't return, it could go on quite a while before it was heeded. Cook could yell herself blue around the gills by then.

"Hahneeweemahneemo," he crooned. "O Idol of the Flies, you have served me true, yea, yea, double yea, forty-five, thirty-two."

Pruitt helped himself to a heaping spoonful of sugar.

The pinkish sky was filled with cawing rooks. They pivoted and wheeled, they planed their wings into black fans and settled in the great old beeches to shout gossip at one another.

Pruitt scuffed his shoe on the stone steps and wished he had an air rifle. He would ask for one on his birthday. He would ask for a lot of impossible things first and then— pitifully—say, "Well, then, could I just have a little old air rifle?" Aunt would fall for that. She was as dumb as his mother had been. Dumber. His mother had been "simple" dumb, which was pretty bad—going in, as she had, for treacly bedtime stories and lap sitting. Aunt was "sick" dumb, which was very dumb indeed. "Sick" dumb people always looked at the "bright side." They were the dumbest of all. They were pushovers, "sick" dumb people were. Easy, little old pushovers.

Pruitt shifted his position as there came to his ears the scrape of footsteps in the hall.

That dragging sound would be cook. He wondered if she really had pulled the muscles loose in her back. Here came Harry with the car. They must be going to the doctor. Harry's hunch made him look like he had a pillow behind him.

"We mustn't let Pruitt know about the string," he heard his aunt say. "It would make him feel badly to learn that he had been the cause."

Cook made a low, unintelligible reply.

"Purposely!" his aunt exclaimed aghast. "Why, Bertha, I'm ashamed of you. He's only a child."

Pruitt drew his lips into a thin line. If she told about the nut hulls, he'd fix her. He scrambled up the steps and held open the screen door.

But cook didn't tell about the nut hulls. She was too busy gritting her teeth against the tearing pull in her back.

"Can I help?" Pruitt let a troubled catch into his voice.

His aunt patted his cheek. "We can manage, dear, thank you."

Miss Bittner smiled on him benevolently. "You can take care of me while they're gone," she said. "We'll have a picnic supper. Won't that be fun?"

"Yes, Miss Bittner. Oodles of fun."

He watched the two women assist their injured companion down the steps with Harry collaborating. He kissed his fingers to his aunt as the car drove away and linked his arm through Miss Bittner's. He gazed cherubically up at her.

"You are a filthy mess," he said caressingly, "and I hate your guts."

Miss Bittner beamed on him. It wasn't often that Pruitt was openly loving to her. "I'm sorry, Pruitt, but I can't hear very well now, you know. Perhaps you'd like me to read to you for a while."

Pruitt shook his head. "I'll just play," he said loudly and distinctly and then, softly, "You liverless old hyena."

"Play?" said Miss Bittner.

Pruitt nodded.

"All right, darling. But don't go far. It'll be suppertime soon."

"Yes, Miss Bittner." He ran lightly down the steps. "Good-by." he called, "you homely, dear, old hag, you."

"Good-by," said Miss Bittner, nodding and smiling.

Pruitt placed the bread board on the pegs and arranged the candles in a semicircle. One of them refused to stay vertical. It had been stepped on.

Pruitt examined it angrily. You'd think she'd be particular with other people's property. The sniveling fool. He'd fix her. He ate the candy rosette with relish and, after it was completely devoured, chewed up the candle, spitting out the wick when it had reached a sufficiently malleable state. He delved into his shirt front and extracted the coal-tar fly which had developed a decided list to starboard. He compressed it into shape, reanchored a wobbly pipestem leg, and established the figure in the center of the bread board.

He folded his arms and began to rock back and forth, the swelling candles spreading his shadow behind him like a thick, dark cloak.

"Hahneeweemahneemo. O Idol of the Flies, hear, hear, O hear, come close and hear. Miss Bittner scrooched one of your candles. So send me lots of flies, lots and lots of flies, millions, trillions, skillions of flies. Quadrillions and skin-tillions. Make them also no-color so's I can mix them up in soup and things without them showing much. Black ones show. Send me pale ones that don't buzz and have feelers.

Hear me, hear me, hear me, O Idol of the Flies, come close and hear!"

Pruitt chewed his candle and contemplated. His face lighted, as he was struck with a brilliant thought. "And make a not-thinking-time-dream-thing hold still so's I can get it. So's I'll know. I guess that's all. Hahneeweemah-neemo, O Idol of the Flies, you are free to GO!"

As he had done earlier in the afternoon, Pruitt became quiescent. His eyes, catlike, were set and staring, staring, staring, staring fixedly at nothing at all.

He didn't look excited. He looked like a small boy engaged in some innocuous small-boyish pursuit. But he was excited. Excitement coursed through his veins and rang in his ears. The pit of his stomach was cold with it and the palms of his hands were as moist as the inside of his mouth was dry.

This was the way he had felt when he knew his father and mother were going to die. He had known it with a sort of clear, glittering lucidity—standing there in the white Bermuda sunlight, waving good-by to them. He had seen the plumy feather on his mother's hat, the sprigged organdy dress, his father's pointed mustache and his slender, artist's hands grasping the driving reins. He had seen the gleaming harness, the high-spirited shake of the horse's head, its stamping foot. His father wouldn't have a horse that wasn't high-spirited. Ginger had been its name. He had seen the bobbing fringe on the carriage top and the pin in the right rear wheel—the pin that he had diligently and with patient perseverance worked loose with the screwdriver out of his toy toolchest. He had seen them roll away, down the drive, out through the wrought iron gates. He had wondered if they would turn over when they rounded the bend and what sort of a crash they would make. They had turned over but he hadn't heard the crash. He had been in the house eating the icing off the cake.

But he had known they were going to die. The knowledge had been almost more than he could control, as even now it was hard to govern the knowledge, the certainty, that he was going to snare a dream-thing.

He knew it. He knew it. He knew it. With every wire-taut nerve in his body he knew it.

Here came one. Streaking through his mind, leaving a string of phosphorescent bubbles in its wake and the bubbles rose and burst and there were dark, bloody smears where they had been. Another—shooting itself along with its tail—its greasy sides ashine. Another—and another—and another—and then a seething whirlpool of them. There had never been so many. Spiny, pulpy, slick and eel-like, some with feelers like catfish, some with white gaping mouths and foreshortened embryo arms. The contortions clogged his thoughts with weeping. But there was one down in the black, not-able-to-get-to part of his mind that watched him. It knew what he wanted. And it was blind. But it was watching him through its blindness. It was coming. Wriggling closer, bringing the black, not-able-to-get-to part with it and where it passed the others sank away and his mind was wild with depraved weeping. Its nose holes went in and out, in and out, in and out, like something he had known long ago in some past, mysterious, other life, and it whimpered as it came and whispered things to him. Disconnected things that swelled his heart and ran like juice along the cracks in his skull. In a moment it would be quite near, in a moment he would know.

"Pruitt, Pruitt." Pollen words, nectareous, sprinkled with flower dust. The dream-thing waited. It did not—like the rest—dart away frightened.

"Pruitt. Pruitt." The voice came from outside himself. From far away and down, from some incredible depth like the place in his mind where They had a nest—only it was distant—and deep. Quite deep. So hot and deep.

With an immense effort Pruitt blinked.

"Look at me." The voice was dulcet and alluring.

Again Pruitt blinked, and as his wits ebbed in like a sluggish tide bringing the watching dream-thing with it, he saw a man.

He stood tall and commanding and from chin to toe he was wrapped in a flowing cape and, in the flickering candlelight, the cape had the exact outlines of Pruitt's shadow, and in and about the cape swam the watching dream-thing as if it were at home. Above the cloak the man's face was a grinning mask, and through the mouth, the nostrils and the slits of eyes poured a reddish translucent light. A glow. Like that of a Halloween pumpkin head, only intensified a thousandfold.

"Pruitt, look, Pruitt." The folds of the cloak lifted and fell as if an invisible arm had gestured. Pruitt followed the gesture hypnotically. His neck twisted round, slowly, slowly, until his gaze encompassed a rain of insects. A living curtain of them. A shimmering and noiseless cascade of colorless flies, gauzy winged, long bodied.

"Flies, Pruitt. Millions of flies."

Pruitt once more rotated his neck until he confronted the stranger. The blind dream-thing giggled at him and swam into a pleat of darkness.

"Who—are—you?" The words were thick and sweet on Pruitt's tongue like other words he half remembered speaking a thousand years ago on some dim plane in some hazy twilight world.

"My name is Asmodeus, Pruitt. Asmodeus. Isn't it a beautiful name?"

"Yes."

"Say it, Pruitt."

"Asmodeus."

"Again."

"Asmodeus."

"Again, Pruitt."

"Asmodeus."

"What do you see in my cloak?"

"A dream-thought."

"And what is it doing?"

"It is gibbering at me."

"Why?"

"Because your cloak has the power of darkness and I may not enter until—"

"Until what, Pruitt?"

"Until I look into your eyes and see—"

"See what, Pruitt?"

"What is written therein."

"And what is written therein? Look into my eyes, Pruitt. Look long and well. What is written therein?"

"It is written what I wish to know. It is written—"

"What is written, Pruitt?"

"It is written of the limitless, the eternal, the foreverness, of the what is and was ordained to ever be, unceasingly, beyond the ends of Time for . . . for—"

"For whom, Pruitt?"

The boy wrenched his eyes away. "No," he said, and in crescendo, "no, no, no, no, no." He scooted backward across the floor, pushing with his hands, shoving with his heels, his face contorted with terror. "No," he babbled, "no, no, no, no, no, no, no, no, no."

"Yes, Pruitt, for whom?"

The boy reached the door and lurched to his feet, his jaw flaccid, his eyes staring in their sockets. He turned and fled up the path, heedless of the pelting flies that fastened themselves to his clothes and tangled in his hair, and touched his flesh like ghostly, clinging fingers, and scrunched beneath his feet as he ran on—his breath breaking from his lungs in sobbing gasps.

"Miss Bittner . . . help . . . Miss Bittner . . . Aunt . . . Harry . . . help—"

At the bend waiting for him stood the figure he had left behind in the bathhouse.

"For whom, Pruitt?"

"No, no, no."

"For whom, Pruitt?"

"No, oh no, no!"

"For whom, Pruitt?"

"For the DAMNED," the boy shrieked and, wheeling, he ran

back the way he had come, the flies sticking to his skin, mashing as he tried frantically to rid himself of them as on he sped.

The man behind him began to chant. High, shrill, and mocking, and the dream-thought took it up, and the earth, and the trees, and the sky that dripped flies, and the pilings of the pier clustered with their pulsating bodies, and the water, patched as far as eye could see with clotted islands of flies, flies, flies. And from his own throat came laughter, crazed and wanton, unrestrained and terrible, peal upon peal of hellish laughter that would not stop. Even as his legs would not stop when they reached the end of the pier.

A red-breasted robin—a fly in its beak—watched the widening ripples. A garden lizard scampered over a tuft of grass and joined company with a toad at the water's edge, as if to lend their joint moral support to the turtle who slid off the bank and with jerky motions of its striped legs went down to investigate the thing that was entwined so securely in a fishing net there on the sandy bottom by the pier.

Miss Bittner idly flipped through a textbook on derivatives. The textbook was a relic of bygone days and the pages were studded with pressed wildflowers brittle with age. With a fingernail she loosened a tissue-thin four-leaf clover. It had left its yellow-green aura on the printed text.

"Beelzebub," Miss Bittner read absently, "stems from the Hebraic. *Beel*—meaning idol, *sebub*—meaning flies: Synonyms, lesser known, not in common usage are: Apollyon, Abbadon, Asmodeus—" but Miss Bittner's attention flagged. She closed the book, yawned and wondered lazily where Pruitt was.

She went to the window and immediately drew back with revulsion. Green Bay flies. Heavens, they were all over everything. The horrid creatures. Funny how they blew in off the water. She recalled last year, when she had been with the Braithwaites in Michigan, they had come—

and in such multitudes that the townspeople had had to shovel them up off the streets. Actually shovel them. She had been ill for three whole days thereafter.

She hoped Pruitt wouldn't be dismayed by them. She must guard against showing her own helpless panic as she had done at teatime. Children placed such implicit faith in the invincibility of their elders.

Dear Pruitt, he had been so charming to her today.

Dear little Pruitt.

The Red-Headed Murderess

✿ BY ROBERT BRANSON

IN WEST China when they bury the dead they heap the grave over with a round mound of earth. The cemeteries bulge with fat, grassy knobs.

There is such a cemetery at the edge of the northern Szechwan town of Hsingping, where I stepped off a river boat one rainy afternoon last September. The cemetery starts at the boat landing and curves down along the river. It lies under a long canopy of old trees. The grass on the graves is very green because there is so much dampness.

I had made the trip all the way from Shanghai to see a geologist named Hank Tyler who had been prospecting for oil two or three years up there. Since he had no idea when I was arriving, he was not at the wharf to meet me. I hired the only taxi in sight—a shabby old sedan.

The driver had considerable trouble getting the car started. It was fitted out to burn charcoal instead of gasoline, and he had to do something complicated to a stovelike contraption that was bolted on behind. I sat on the lumpy back seat, my clothes soggy with sweat and rain, and looked out into the cemetery.

I saw a man sitting there, about a hundred yards away,

beside a grave at the edge of the river. The grave had a white cross on top. The man's outline was dimmed by mist and drizzle, but he was wearing a black Western suit and one of those U.S. Army sun helmets. I knew at once that he must be a Christian missionary paying homage to some departed Christian soul. From an old American lady in Shanghai, I had learned that there were two missionaries in Hsingping—a Reverend Sprague and a Reverend Fitzgibbons, one American, one English. The old lady, in fact, had insisted on giving me some table doilies for their wives.

The driver was still puttering with the charcoal burner. I leaned through the window and asked him who the man in the cemetery was. "Over there"—I pointed—"is that Mr. Sprague? Is that the *megwa* missionary?"

The driver grinned and nodded and said something in Chinese I didn't understand. I wasn't convinced.

"Is it Mr. Fitzgibbons?"

He grinned and nodded again.

"Which one?"

"Yes, sir."

After a minute or two more of this, I gave up. I unstrapped my bag, dug out the package, and walked into the cemetery. I had neither umbrella nor raincoat, but I knew I could scarcely get any wetter than I already was. And the sooner I could get this errand out of the way, the better.

The sod was mushy underfoot and water dripped from the trees. As I approached, I could see that the man beside the Christian grave was drenched. He sat on a bamboo stool with his back to the flat, muddy water of the river, and his hands were folded in his lap. Drops of rain hung from the rim of his sun helmet. Certainly, I thought, this was above and beyond even a missionary's duties.

He watched me as I stepped along between the great humps of earth. He was young, not more than thirty. He had a thin bony face and a jutting Adam's apple. He wore steel-rimmed spectacles. His shirt was filthy and he needed a shave badly. Behind his spectacles, his eyes were dark and unfriendly. He neither smiled at me nor got up.

"Reverend Sprague?" I asked.

"Yes, I'm Sprague." His voice was as solemn as his face.

"I thought it might be you. I'm up here to visit Mr. Tyler. Before I left Shanghai, an acquaintance of yours—a Mrs. Crabbe—gave me something to pass along to your wife."

"That was thoughtful of Mrs. Crabbe," he replied very slowly, still not smiling. "She must not know that my wife was taken with cholera nearly a year ago." He nodded at the white cross. There was an awkward silence for a moment.

"I'm sorry," I said. "Well, I wish you'd take this package anyway. I think it's some table linen. Half of it's for you and the rest is for Mrs. Fitzgibbons. I'd appreciate it if you'd give it to her next time you see her and tell her where it came from."

Real pain seemed to creep into his dark eyes. His lips moved a little, but he said nothing.

"Mrs. Crabbe said everyone up here would know Mrs. Fitzgibbons," I said. "A woman with bright red hair."

Sprague looked down at the ground. I couldn't see his face.

"God forgive me for what I say, if He can," he said. "I wish that Mrs. Fitzgibbons were dead. I wish that she and her red hair and her blue beads and her husband were all in hell."

Hank Tyler told me about the Spragues and the Fitzgibbonses that night as we sat on his veranda, smoking. Below us, the fires and lamps of the town swam through a curtain of drizzle.

"Sprague and his wife came out here from somewhere in the Middle West right after the war. He's a Christian missionary and this was his first overseas assignment. She was one pretty girl—long black hair and big brown eyes and a skin like peaches and cream. She couldn't have been more than twenty-two or so. They'd just been married, and Sprague was crazy about her. He was utterly and completely infatuated.

"She died during a cholera epidemic about six months later, and Sprague's been a little off his rocker ever since. He's there in the cemetery like that every day."

I asked Hank where the Fitzgibbonses fitted into the picture. He replied that Sprague held the Englishman and his wife responsible for the death. He lighted a cigarette.

"The Fitzes were old-timers out here," he said. "They had a big comfortable house with plenty of servants. When the Spragues landed in Hsingping in 1946, they didn't have any place to stay. The Fitzes persuaded them to move in with them.

"The cholera epidemic broke out about six months later. Sprague himself was away at the time—up-country on some kind of religious expedition. He didn't know anything about his wife's illness until he got back. That was three or four days after she died.

"Sprague found the village full of cholera and the Fitzes' house deserted. Mr. and Mrs. Fitz had cleared out to Chungking and left only a note behind them. The note explained how they'd done their best for poor Mrs. Sprague, and how they'd given her a fine burial, and that they were going to Chungking until the epidemic blew over.

"It nearly killed Sprague. The servants found him lying in the courtyard having some sort of fit. They put him to bed, and nursed him along with Chinese snake medicine, and finally he came out of it after about a week. I think he'd kill the Fitzes now if he ever got his hands on them."

"You can't hold anyone responsible for cholera," I suggested.

"No, you don't hold anyone responsible for cholera," Hank replied. "Sprague's completely irrational about the whole thing, of course. Like I told you, he's off his rocker.

But I'll tell you something odd about it: I think he's righter than he knows."

Hank flicked the stub of his cigarette over the veranda railing and its red coal fell out of sight in a long slow arc through the rain. "Everyone here in the town is convinced that the Fitzes—or Mrs. Fitz, really—did the girl in with a hatchet. Pure murder."

"On what evidence?" I asked.

"Lots of it," he answered. "For one thing, the Fitzes never came back. They've dropped completely out of sight. But there's more to it than that."

This is what Hank told me: The Reverend Fitzgibbons was a big jovial Englishman of about fifty. His body was heavy with ale and overeating and years of leisure. Gardening was his most strenuous activity. He had a tremendous booming laugh, and everyone liked him.

"Jolly is probably the word for him," Hank said.

His wife could scarcely have resembled him less. Mrs. Fitzgibbons was waspish in both size and disposition. Her face was tiny and sharp, her mouth a thin straight line, her voice shrill. Her whole being was bent on destroying "filth," both physical and spiritual, and she ruled her husband, her servants, and the parishioners with a puritanical fury.

"I think she smiled once a year," Hank said. "Lord, but she was 'good.' "

She dressed austerely—long black or gray dresses, utterly plain; black cotton stockings; "sensible" shoes. Her only traces of plumage were her hair, which was a vivid carroty red, and a string of blue glass beads which had been her mother's and which she wore constantly. Because of her phobia about filth, she never left the mission compound without first masking her face in veils that hung from a black straw bonnet.

"She'd go to the market every morning looking like something out of H. G. Wells," Hank said. "You couldn't see her face—just a great gauze head."

When the Spragues came to town and moved in with the Fitzes, everything went well for a time.

"But after two or three months," Hank said, "the two women began feuding. Sprague's wife, as I've told you, was a really luscious young thing. Mrs. Fitz wouldn't like that. Apparently, she started nursing a little coal of jealousy. She started making the most embarrassing kind of accusations—claiming that Sprague's wife was making eyes at the Reverend Fitz, and so on.

"I don't know just how the coal grew—and it's not really too important—but apparently it developed into a white-hot, really pathological hatred. Things got to the point where Mrs. Fitz refused to talk to Mrs. Sprague, or even eat at the same table. The servants say she ordered the Spragues out of the house a dozen times. Sprague was making arrangements for a new house when he had to go up-country on that expedition.

"The servants claim none of them saw Mrs. Sprague the day she died. The cholera epidemic had been on about a week. The Reverend Fitz came down to the kitchen in the morning and told the cook to fix breakfast trays and a basin of scalding water. He said that Mrs. Sprague had come down with cholera in the night, and that he and Mrs. Fitz were staying at the bedside. He ordered none of the servants to come upstairs because of the danger of contagion.

"Early in the afternoon he came down for more food. He shook his head and looked glum, and told the staff that Mrs. Sprague was getting worse, and ordered one of the boys to ride to a village thirty miles away to fetch an American doctor. We figured afterward that this was just pure camouflage; Fitz knew damned well it would take at least twenty-four hours before the doctor could get to Hsing-ping."

I interrupted. "But I don't quite get this," I said. "You said Fitz was a good egg. Why should he want to murder the girl?"

"Undoubtedly he didn't," Hank said. "But that witch of a wife ruled him like a child. How she worked herself up to the act of murder is a question for a psychiatrist. But once the deed was done, she must have persuaded old Fitz to stick by her and cover up. The way we piece the thing together, Mrs. Sprague was lying dead all day up there in the bedroom. Mrs. Fitz probably did the job before daylight. And she and Fitz were standing guard over the body until night fell again.

"Anyway," Hank continued, "Fitz came downstairs a third time about eleven o'clock that night. He woke up the servants and told them that Mrs. Sprague, rest her soul, had expired. He gave two of the boys a wad of money and told them to wake up the coffinmaker down the street and bring a coffin back to the mission house at once. Then they were to go to the cemetery and begin preparing a grave; the burial must take place as soon as possible in the interest of the public health. Another boy was to go to the boatmen's quarter and hire a sampan for a trip downriver. The cook was to boil another kettle of water. And none of the servants was to pass beyond the foot of the stairs.

"The coffin arrived. Fitz lugged it upstairs himself. An hour later he came to the head of the stairs and called for the boys. The coffin was in one of the bedrooms, and its lid had already been nailed down snug. The boys got it downstairs and took it to the cemetery on a bull cart. Fitz stood by with a lantern, giving a running funeral oration, while they spaded it over with soil.

"That's about all there was to it. An hour or two before dawn, Fitz sent for two rickshas. He and Mrs. Fitz got into one, all bundled up for traveling, and the boys piled their luggage into the other. The sampan shoved off for Chungking, and no one's seen hide nor hair of the Fitzes since.

"They did send Sprague a note from the coast some weeks later. They said they had decided not to return to Hsingping—sadness of the memories, or something. They said they were making a new start, and told Sprague to take

over their house if he liked. The letter didn't have any
return address on it, only a Hong Kong postmark.

"But the rumors didn't really begin to circulate until one
of the servants stumbled across a roll of bloodstained bed-
clothes and a hatchet. They'd been stuffed through a crack
into a space between two walls, and it was pure miracle
that they were ever discovered at all."

"Does Sprague know about that?"

"No," Hank said. "And no one in the village would think
of telling him. He is much pitied."

I've had these details set down in my notebook for nearly
a year now. It struck me they were ideal ingredients for a
story. Jealousy and hatred among the missionaries. A pious
murderess with red hair and a blue necklace. Death by
hatchet in an upper bedroom, and a hasty burial by lan-
ternlight in a Chinese cemetery. The grief-crazed devotion
of a missionary who sits in all weather by the riverside
grave of his bride—but who knows less about her death
than the village gossips.

I've been intending to do a story for months. But I didn't
have the ending for it until yesterday. I got a letter from
Hank Tyler. It was a long letter, the bulk of it devoted to
data for a series of articles I'm doing on China. Toward the
end of the letter, Hank wrote:

"You may have read about the floods in Szechwan last
month. Five people died here in the village and the damage
was tremendous. One of those who died was Sprague, the
missionary, whom I'm sure you remember. The man in the
cemetery. He got soaked wading around and died of pneu-
monia before anyone knew he was sick. He's undoubtedly
happier dead, poor man. The flood brought his story to a
nasty little finish in more ways than one.

"You'll remember that the cemetery was right beside the
river. Well, the water spilled over into the cemetery and for
a couple of days it pounded through there in a regular
torrent. When the flood finally subsided, the cemetery was

a mess. There was a good foot of mud and rocks and wreck-age over everything, and about twenty of the graves had been washed out.

"They found Sprague's wife's coffin half buried in silt with part of the lid battered off. You know what they found inside? Some red hair and a string of blue beads. . . ."

The Language of Flowers

§ BY HUGH ATKINSON

GOD hands out sensibility, like beauty, in very unequal measures. It is an endowment essential to the poet. In the politician or encyclopaedia salesman, sensibility is like a wen on the nose. Mr. Herman, had he been asked, would have added bank manager to these last two categories.

To be gifted with such a fine comprehension of feeling, an empathy so extraordinary, that one finds oneself transferred inside the skin of every chance contact and acquaintance, is an awkward condition in a world which provides that a man must look out for himself. In a bank manager dealing with mortgages and loans, it is as onerous as it is unparalleled. In his youth Mr. Herman suffered many painful interviews with his low-sensibility superiors. Only by the dint of practice and the nagging of his wife did he manage sufficient discipline to continue employed to the age of retirement at his uncomfortable, unchosen profession. Mr. Herman had never expected to be condemned to a bank. He had expected to be a vintner. His German ancestors, a hundred years before, had settled in the Barossa Valley. There, with other Germans who had fled religious persecution, the Hermans ate German food, sang German songs, married other Germans, and sowed German grape vines brought from the Rhône on the sun-dappled Barossa slopes. The vines were green and the wine was red and there were many German festivals and feast days. Great-grandfather Herman and Grandfather Herman, who had both died without having spoken English, flourished there as vintners. But Father Herman, like Omar Khayyám, could find no goods he bought halfway as precious as the casks of wine that he sold. He applied himself to consuming his product, which scandalized his Lutheran brethren, and when he was carried off as pickled and reeking as the timbers of his own winesoaked barrels, he left behind a neglected vineyard and an account of his debts in a ledger recorded in Teutonic detail.

His father's decline pained his son's sensibility but he couldn't help understanding his father. When an uncle arranged for him to enter the bank, even though the prospect dismayed him, young Herman recognized that his motives were the best and put on a good face for his uncle's sake.

But the feeling for the vines and the smell of turned earth were too deep to be eradicated by figures. For forty-five years Herman went to his duties like a man to his execution. And returned home at night to the gardens he made, like a man who had been given a reprieve. Mr. Herman's gardens were a wonder to see and it tore his heart to leave them. But wherever the bank posted him next, he would start a new garden first thing. Always, no matter how calamitous the climate or soil, Mr. Herman would put down a grape vine.

It was a great day and a great relief when Mr. Herman got a branch of his own. Even though it wasn't much more than a room in the newest suburb of Adelaide.

"At last," he told the wife he had married from the Barossa, "at last I can put down my roots. This will be my last garden."

His wife said, "First, last, what's the difference? Some-

times I think if I watered you, Herman, put you in a hole up
to your ankles and took the can and gave you a watering,
next morning I'd find you standing there with green shoots
coming out of your ears."

His wife called her husband Herman because his Christian name was Adolph. In the war it had been an embarrassment. When he gave his name, Mr. Herman knew exactly what others were thinking.

Herman had managed his branch for ten years when he
got a call to the head office. In a growing state, bountiful
with resources, suburbs and banks grow too. The staff director, who had every reason to be familiar with Herman's
history, sat behind a big desk in a panelled room and
greeted Herman with unnecessary exuberance. Herman
could detect by his face and manner that the director was
not at ease. His handshake was overhearty and he seemed
troubled about the eyes. Herman thought: "The poor fellow
has something unpleasant to say. After all these years,
doing this job, unpleasantness still causes him pain." He
overlooked, feeling for the staff director, that any unpleasantness exchanged in the room would unhesitatingly de-
volve on himself.

"Must be five years since we last saw each other," the
staff director said.

Herman considered. Apart from his weakness of sensibility, he was scrupulously accurate at figures.

"Four years and seven months on the twenty-third. It was
at the Christmas party."

"So it was, so it was." The director seemed delighted with
the information.

Mr. Herman waited.

"Business seems to be growing out your way."

"Deposits have increased eight hundred and thirty-two
percent," Herman said. "Loans have increased—"

"Yes, yes," the director said. "Did you know there's a car
plant going up, out there?"

"I had heard a rumor."

"The company expects to employ fifteen hundred to begin. This means a great deal of new settlement. Shops, homes, buildings and so on."

"Loans?" Mr. Herman said.

"Loans and mortgages," the staff director said firmly.

Herman thought of his garden. A ten-year garden. The best and biggest he had ever made.

"You're not thinking of posting me?"

"We're thinking of retiring you."

"Retiring? But I've got five years to go."

"Why wait five years? We've worked out a scheme. Look, here are the figures."

When Mr. Herman left the room, slightly dazed, it had been established that his retirement would begin one calendar month from that day.

Mr. Herman went home to tell his wife. When she recovered from the shock she was first concerned about the cut he had to take in his pension. But Herman explained that it was a small deprivation.

"Ach," she said, returning to her childhood tongue as she sometimes did in emotion, "we can go back to the Barossa and get a small house."

Herman blinked through his glasses.

"No," he said, "we will stay right here. I'm not going to start a new garden."

He appreciated his wife's feelings. But he had been doing things her way all their married life and now he wanted something his way.

At the bank he conveyed the news to his staff and was touched to see in their faces that the routine expressions of loss and good wishes were heartfelt and unaffected.

When Colonel Cleary heard about it from the teller, he marched into Herman's office.

"What the blazes is this, about your retiring?"

"You know the old saying. Retire while you can still enjoy it."

"Stuff and nonsense," said Colonel Cleary, "you're hardly

more than a boy. I suppose they'll replace you with some young pup with no idea how to deal with a gentleman."

Colonel Cleary looked like a cartoon colonel. He had carried a lance in a cavalry charge on the Indian frontier in 1918. Retired to Australia on a miserable pension, he had found in Herman an understanding banker who never troubled his pride when he needed an overdraft between one pension cheque and another. Being chronically strapped, as he used to put it, with no regiments left to command, it was important to Colonel Cleary that someone should treat him with respect. Mr. Herman not only listened to his stories but handled his account personally, as though the Colonel was his biggest depositor.

On the morning of Herman's last day at the bank, the Colonel struggled in with a package. It was wrapped in crepe paper and made an unusual shape.

"Small gesture," said the Colonel, looking red and fierce to camouflage his feelings. "Mark of appreciation, do y'see?"

"What is it?" asked Herman, putting on his glasses.

"Vanda Coerulea, hybridized. Parent plant comes from Northern India. Grows on the uplands with a preference for full sunlight on small trees sparse in the foliage."

He undid the paper.

"There," he said, "grew it myself."

A spike of magnificent orchid blooms nodded in the draught from the door.

Mr. Herman caught his breath.

"How very, very beautiful."

Like exotic birds suspended in flight, the unearthly blue of the blossoms, patterned boldly in darker checks, continued to nod and shiver.

Mr. Herman said: "Has it a perfume?"

"What's the time?" asked the Colonel.

Herman looked at the wall clock.

He said: "Twenty-three minutes to ten."

"You wouldn't notice it now. Too early. Sun's not high enough yet."

Herman said: "I don't understand."

"Perfectly simple," said the Colonel. "The plant's not mad, y'know. Puts out perfume when the insects are about so that pollination sets during the heat of the day."

"How very extraordinary," Herman said.

"See these leaves?" The Colonel touched the long green straps that spread like a cobra's hood. "They always point from east to west. If you turn the ruddy thing north and south the leaves grow east and west again."

"I don't know what to say," Herman said; "I've never owned an orchid before."

"The ruddy things talk to you when y'get to know 'em. That replacement of yours arrived yet?"

Herman said: "We were introduced yesterday."

"If he don't come up to scratch I'll move my account, you can tell him that, whoever he is."

The Colonel put his hand out.

"Good-bye and good luck and I don't mind telling you, I'm ruddy sorry to see you go."

There was a little party in the bank after closing. Mr. Herman went home with a silver tray as well as the *Vanda Coerulea*. In his garden he looked about and expelled a long breath. The daily reprieves for which he had lived now stretched before him forever.

In the living room he stationed the orchid behind the sliding glass doors.

Mrs. Herman said: "I don't like it. It looks thoroughly evil."

"It's beautiful," her husband said. "How can a flower be evil?"

"It's a nasty, jungly thing," said Mrs. Herman, narrowing her eyes at the plant. "It's bad enough spending all your time in the garden. I won't have you bringing the garden inside."

Herman said: "Orchids need humidity. This one comes from India."

"Never liked Indians," said Mrs. Herman, who had never met an Indian in her life. "It can stay here tonight, but tomorrow morning out in the garden it goes."

"Tomorrow morning," Herman said, "just imagine, tomorrow morning."

Mrs. Herman looked suspicious.

"What about tomorrow morning?"

"I don't have to go to the bank."

"If you think you're going to spend all your time in the garden, you're very much mistaken. The guttering needs cleaning and the house is a sight. It needs painting inside and out."

In the kitchen she banged the pots about. "Retired," Herman heard her say, "retired at his age. Women can't retire. Cooking and cleaning go on forever."

Next day Mrs. Herman went into Adelaide, shopping. Pulling on her gloves she told her husband: "When I get back I don't want to see that thing."

Herman sat behind the glass, warmed by the sun, and read the paper after she left. There was something about the orchid that made him uneasy and he put down the paper to study it. It seemed to Herman that the blooms had changed color. The unearthly blue had paled.

He said: "I don't believe you're quite happy. Perhaps it's too hot next to the glass."

He moved the pot back where the sun mixed with shadows and returned to the gardening notes. Mr. Herman never read the rest of the paper. The human disasters celebrated in the press always caused him pain and confusion. When he had finished he glanced at the orchid.

"Well, I'm blessed," he said.

In its sheltered position the plant had got its color back.

"You like that, do you?" said Herman.

The *Vanda Coerulea* nodded on its spike.

While he washed the breakfast dishes left by his wife, Mr. Herman pondered on the flower. There was no doubt she would not have it inside and no doubt that it must have a shelter.

"I'll build it a glasshouse, that's what I'll do," Mr. Herman suddenly decided. With his hands in the dishwater he felt a lift of excitement. The more he thought about it, the better the idea seemed. He couldn't wait to get started. He chipped the good milk jug through not looking what he was doing, while the glasshouse grew in his mind.

"I'm going to build you a house of your own, what do you think of that?" he said to the *Vanda Coerulea*. Watching the plant, something troubled him and then the sun caught his eye.

"There's something wrong," he said, "but I just can't put my finger on it."

He looked at the sun again. "Rises in the east, sets in the west," he said thoughtfully. "Of course. That's it. I've got you turned the wrong way."

The straplike leaves that spread like a cobra's hood were slightly out of order.

Herman said: "East to west's the thing. It must be most uncomfortable the other way, and very tiring and painful."

As he leaned back on his heels, at a level with the blooms, his nose pricked on something strange. The odor was fragile, yet disturbingly fetid and sweet. Mr. Herman sniffed and wrinkled his nose and looked about at the heavy, plain furniture. There were vases of jonquils, cinerarias, gardenias, and carnations arranged in the room. None of these accounted for the foreign bridling of Mr. Herman's olfactory nerves. Almost reluctantly, he bent over the *Vanda Coerulea*. As he did, the plant emitted a wave of perfume so heavy it made him splutter.

"I'll be damned," Mr. Herman said, and cleared his nose in a handkerchief. He remembered what Colonel Cleary had told him. "You're all mixed up," he said to the orchid. "It's only nine o'clock." Imperceptibily, the strange burden of perfume withdrew and faded from the room.

"Now what's up?" Herman said. "What the devil has

gone wrong now?" He put his face to the blooms and sniffed his nose hard. There wasn't a trace of perfume. At last, shyly, he began to smile. "I do believe you were trying to thank me," he said, "the way the marmalade cat purrs when I scratch him."

Mr. Herman had difficulty concentrating his thoughts when he sat down to draw up the glasshouse. The ghost of the perfume haunted his nostrils and the flower drew his eyes like blue flame.

He could build the orchid house in a day, using precut timber and glass. But the materials would require time to prepare, leaving the *Vanda* unsheltered. A garage would have served for a night or two, but Herman owned no garage. He did have a car. With the back seat removed the *Vanda Coerulea* would fit in the car quite snugly. Happily Herman picked up the pencil and began expertly to make calculations.

It took a long time to find a timber merchant who could execute the order immediately. And more time finding a glazier who stocked the glass he required. It was late afternoon when Herman got off the bus that stopped at the end of his street. Mrs. Herman had returned from town. The car was in the drive. Mr. Herman decided to experiment. When he got the back seat out he found three and eightpence in coins, nine hairpins, a lipstick, and a packet of ten squashed cigarettes of a brand departed from the market. Herman cleaned up carefully and put the seat back in its place. He reminded himself to wind down a front window so that the *Vanda* would get air without draught. He was disturbed that his wife might have already moved the orchid, feeling about it as she did. Perhaps north to south, or, worse, out of the house altogether.

The orchid was positioned as he had left it. But the blooms hung sad and pale.

"Did you touch that orchid?" Herman demanded, before he had fairly got into the room.

"Are you addressing me?" Mrs. Herman said dangerously.

"Who do you think I'm addressing? I asked did you touch that orchid?"

Mrs. Herman looked at her husband to the plant and back again.

"I wouldn't touch the beastly thing with a stick. Where have you been to this hour?"

"Then why has it lost color?" Herman said with excitement, ignoring his wife's interrogative.

"Lost color?" she said, fairly put out and widening her eyes at her husband.

"You can hear me can't you?" Herman shouted. "You understand English don't you?"

"A little better then the Hermans, since you've brought it up. It's the Hermans who are famous for taking three generations to get their tongues around an English word."

Mr. Herman lost his bearings in this sudden switch of subject.

He said: "What are you talking about?"

"What are YOU talking about?" Mrs. Herman inquired. "Coming in at six in the evening babbling about flowers losing color."

On the track again now Herman glanced at the *Vanda Coerulea.* Then he removed his spectacles. And replaced them on his nose. While he watched, the orchid flushed its petals. In a minute the blooms were erect on their petals, glowing more unearthly than ever.

"I asked you where you've been? Get that thing out of the house. Who chipped my good milk jug?"

Even though she said everything at once it made no impression on Herman. He contemplated the *Vanda,* with wonderment on his face.

Mrs. Herman felt uneasy and the sound of her voice gave her comfort.

She said: "I've heard that retired men go senile but I didn't expect it in twenty-four hours."

She said: "Spending money on a glasshouse when every room needs repainting."

She said: "Can't be trusted to wash up without breaking the crockery."

After they had eaten and Herman returned after removing the *Vanda Coerulea,* Mrs. Herman waited until it was time for "In Your Garden" on TV. Then she changed the station to "News and Newsreel" and sat down doggedly to watch it. Ordinarily, when he upset her, Herman was sorry and made an apology. Now he got up and prepared for bed. He said nothing about "In Your Garden."

When the glass and timber was delivered next day, Herman immediately set to work. His wife watched from the house as he hammered furiously, without stopping for a cup of tea.

"I don't know what's got into that man," she thought as she hoovered the carpet. Where the orchid had stood there was a stain from the pot. It made her more angry than ever.

Herman only picked at his salad lunch and afterward almost ran down the path. In the afternoon he had to return twice for Band-Aids to stick on his cut fingers.

It was dark when he finished. "There you are. What do you think of that?" he asked peering anxiously at the flower in the gloom. He stood watching until his wife called him.

In the next month Herman divided his time between painting and sitting in the glasshouse. Relations with his wife were amicable enough as long as he was up the ladder. When he visited the orchid she showed signs of temper. Herman had formed the habit of drinking his morning tea in the glasshouse, carrying it there in a pottery mug. The *Vanda* was putting out perfume when Mrs. Herman brought him letters to post. She had no sooner introduced her head than the perfume went out like a light. And no sooner withdrawn, with certain expressions of distaste, than the orchid perfumed the air again with unmistakable deliberation.

"You are a naughty thing," Herman chided. But felt pleased, nevertheless.

All his adult life Herman's sensibility had been cheated of proper fulfilment. In his communion with the *Vanda* there was no obstacle of words to confuse their triumphant understanding. No meanness of ego or interest, no inequality of spirit or feeling to blight their perfect rapport. The imperceptible language by which they communicated was a precious thing in itself. The orchid depended utterly on the refinement of his understanding. As a child learns words to declare its wants, Herman learned the *Vanda's* vocabulary. The long roots that had scrambled outside the pot, like a horrible daddy-longlegs, his wife said, went white and transparent when the *Vanda* was thirsty. Herman would measure out water until the roots turned green at the tips.

He neglected his glorious garden to spend more time in the company of the orchid. Mrs. Herman took to complaining about this, although she had resented the garden before. Relations between them became painfully strained. Sometimes Herman found himself comparing his wife to the orchid. And decided that she was a hefty Hausfrau, coarse and vulgar in her feelings.

One day, when he had gone to buy paint, Herman met Colonel Cleary.

"I'm shifting my account," the Colonel said. "That ruddy replacement of yours is an out-and-out untouchable. How's the orchid?"

"She doesn't seem herself," Herman said.

"Oh? What's the trouble?"

"I don't quite know."

"Any fungus? Red spider? Snails?"

Mr. Herman looked surprised.

"Of course not. She would have mentioned it."

"Mentioned it?" said the Colonel.

"Undoubtedly," Herman said. "She would have let me know immediately."

He pondered.

"I can't help wondering if she wants to breed."

The Colonel looked hard at Herman. "Do you know how to cross an orchid?"

"I could ask her, I suppose."

"Ask who?"

"Just ask," Herman said vaguely.

The Colonel said: "If you come over to the house I'll show you how to do it."

"I should get back," Herman said, "she looked very peaked this morning."

"Sorry to hear it," the Colonel said, thinking about Herman's wife.

"I believe I will, if you'd be so kind," Mr. Herman decided.

"Will what?"

"Come over to the house."

Colonel Cleary lived with his married daughter in a small flat separated from the house. In the bed-sitting-room, decorated with military trophies, they sat down over a spike of orchids.

"Here's what y'do," said the Colonel. "See this?" He indicated the flower's center. "This is the lip. The canoe-shaped protuberance over the lip is what we call the column. There's a little cap just here on the column. You break it off with your fingers, like this do y'see, and there are the two pollinia."

The fleshy cap, which had come away as neatly as a helmet, exposed two yellow seeds half the size of a match head.

The Colonel picked them off with a toothpick.

"You take the pollinia and squeeze them under here, on the anther."

Mr. Herman said: "Is that all?"

"That's all. After conception two fine cords grow down from the anther to the ovary. When the stem below the flowerhead swells, you know the ruddy thing is pregnant."

Mr. Herman took off his glasses, wiped them, and scratched in his thinning hair.

He said: "Very sexy, isn't it?"

The Colonel said: "You need something with size and texture to cross with that *Vanda* you've got. Something rounded, with meat in the petals, to build up her ruddy figure a bit."

"What would you suggest?"

"I've got a *Cimbidium* outside called Falstaff, I could let you have for a fiver."

The Colonel was being chronically strapped and getting no help from Herman's replacement.

"You're sure he'd be right for her?"

"You couldn't do better," the Colonel said. "Should get something pretty good out of it."

When Mr. Herman got back to the glasshouse the *Vanda* seemed in good spirits. He decided to wait to introduce her to Falstaff and put the new orchid under the bench. Mr. Herman wasn't greatly taken with Falstaff. The flower was blotched red, heavy and gross, and recovering from a touch of the fungus. The Colonel had given Herman a bottle of poison with which Falstaff needed to be sprayed. "Be ruddy careful," he had warned, "orchid poisons are deadly dangerous. Don't smoke when you're using it and give your hands a ruddy good scrubbing afterwards."

There was trouble when Herman went up to the house. He had forgotten to buy the paint.

Next morning, as was usual, he took his mug of tea and visited the glasshouse.

"I've got something for you," he told the *Vanda* and produced Falstaff from under the bench. He put the two pots together. The *Vanda* looked utterly blank. Herman dosed her with fertilized water and waited until the roots glistened green.

"I suppose I had better give you a spraying," he said to Falstaff. "I don't want you giving her the fungus."

He prepared the poison as he had been instructed and was rather nervous about it. The Colonel had drawn a great skull and crossbones on the bottle.

That evening when he had finished painting, Herman went back to the glasshouse. The roots of the *Vanda,* on Falstaff's side, had climbed away, back into the pot. He moved the new orchid to the end of the bench. Next morning the *Vanda's* roots had assumed their usual pattern.

This time, when he arrived with his tea, he carried a pencil and pad.

While he sipped at the mug he headed a page with the date and made the following note: "I foresee trouble. She has made it plain that my arrangements are not to her liking." Then he picked up Falstaff and put him back alongside the *Vanda.*

Over the following weeks his notes read:

"28 October. Still making no progress."

"3 November. When I came in this morning she turned the most ghastly color."

"6 November. I have tried every way to placate her and am feeling greatly distressed."

"9 November. I should give up trying but her behavior is making me stubborn."

With proper sensitivity, Herman had no wish to impregnate the orchid without, as it were, first obtaining her consent. Not only did she reject her red-blotched mate but gave other signals of jealousy. Herman had noted that when he treated Falstaff with the poison, she changed color, withdrew her scent, or went white at the root tips. In those difficult weeks he several times decided to give up and abandon his intention. But what with the way things were at the house, he found himself cranky.

On 11 November he noted on his pad: "I'm getting fed up being bullied by women."

On 13 November he noted with dismay that the *Vanda* had caught Falstaff's fungus. His entry for that day read: "I wouldn't be surprised if this is her way of blackmail. She knows I'm afraid of the poison."

On 17 November, Mrs. Herman got a letter announcing the engagement of her niece to one of the oldest German families in the Barossa. There would be a house party and Aunt and Uncle Herman were invited to stay the weekend.

Herman said: "You'll have to go on your own."

Mrs. Herman was incredulous.

"Go on my own? To a weekend party? To the engagement of your own niece?"

"I can't get away," Herman said.

"What do you mean you can't get away? Of course you can get away. You're retired. You can get away like anything."

"I can't get away. I'm having trouble with the orchid."

Mrs. Herman blew up. There had never been such a scene. Through it all Herman simply repeated that he was unable to get away. Finally, in a storm of tears, Mrs. Herman locked herself in the bedroom. She didn't know what to do, or where to turn. She was convinced her husband had gone mad.

It was this scene, as much as anything, that forged in Herman the temper of decision.

He was up and striding to the glasshouse before he knew he had moved.

There, he snapped cap after cap off Falstaff's columns, and as brutally as a rapist, pressed home the pollinia on the *Vanda's* shrinking anthers.

He was so upset, when he had finished the act, that he sat in the car and smoked five cigarettes.

After a long time he went back to the house. Mrs. Herman was still locked in the bedroom. He made tea and carried it out. He didn't dare look at the *Vanda,* but got out the poison and gave her fungus a spraying. Then he wrote on the pad: "A sad day. Things between us will never be the same."

The poison trickled down the *Vanda's* spike and collected in the nodes of the leaves. As one node filled the poison spilled out and filled the node below it.

Mr. Herman sat unhappily and stared through the glass at the untended things in his garden.

The pottery cup stood beside the orchid pot. As the last node filled, the leaves that flared from the stem like a cobra's hood slowly changed their east to west alignment. The bottom leaf reached out like a tongue and the poison splashed into the tea.

The big, hard-faced man in the ugly felt hat said to the other big man: "She said she went to her room, after the quarrel, and didn't find him until around two o'clock. She said he'd been acting very strangely."

The other man said: "He made a good job of it. The doctor said he had enough poison in him to kill a horse."

"Never understand suicides," the first man said. "It's hard enough keeping alive, these days."

"He could have been worried by his retirement. It gets some of them like that. They think they must be over the hill."

"I suppose so," the other man said, picking up Mr. Herman's pad.

The first man said: "This blue thing's a fantastic color."

"Holy mackerel," the other man said.

"What is it?"

"Just listen to this: I foresee trouble. She has made it plain my arrangements are not to her liking. . . . 6 November, I have tried every way to placate her and am feeling greatly distressed. . . . 11 November, I'm fed up being bullied by women. . . . 13 November, I wouldn't be surprised if this is her way of blackmail. She knows I'm afraid of the poison. . . ."

"Here, show me that," the first man said. When he had read the notes he repeated: "She knows I'm afraid of the poison. . . ."

The hard-faced man folded the notepaper carefully and put it in an inside pocket.

"Well," he said, "we'd better get up there."

The glasshouse filled with a sweet, fetid perfume.

Ashes to Ashes

✌ BY NUNNALLY JOHNSON

I

AT FIRST, occasionally, Ethel Faber had some misgivings as to the propriety of accepting so many and such expensive gifts from another man, but Ralph himself reassured her. Ralph was her husband. Take them, he said, all that were offered.

As pleased as this made her, she suffered, for the briefest of seconds, a twinge of pain that he should with such callousness ignore the opportunity of flattering her with threats of a wallop on the jaw if ever she accepted another token from August Ehler, but it passed so quickly she failed, then, to perceive the real significance of the incident. She gave herself over entirely to the luxury of these tributes which August stood at her elbow each evening. Soon, in the excess of her pleasure, she had forgotten the pain.

The first of August's gifts—she remembered it for a long, long time—had been a quart of gin, low-grade stuff, the same solution of water, juniper juice and alcohol that Ralph bought and drank steadily. August Ehler was at that

175

time virtually at the outset of his career, working in a small way and among a limited clientele, a far cry indeed from his wealthy and fashionable circle of less than a year later. Boyishly enthusiastic in his ambitions, yet wholly and seriously wrapped up in the fascinating intricacies of his new business, he had engaged first the interest and then the friendship of the Fabers quite as much for the lovable complexity of his personality, at once deeply devout and broadly tolerant, as for the reliability of his gin and the moderateness of his prices. Behind his frank devotion to and reliance on the Gospel, they found a comfort and a feeling of safety which they had been able to discover in no other bootlegger.

They came to trust him with the blind confidence of little children. They would drink, without the faintest hesitation, anything he brought to them—anything. And he, on his part, appreciated their faith and was moved deeply by it. And God willing, he told them many times, they would never regret it.

It became a fond memory to them, the occasion of August's first shy offer of the gin to Ethel.

"Mrs. Faber," he had said, awkwardly ill at ease, looking very much like a tender young curate, "I just brought this extra quart along for you."

He blushed at his own boldness, and sought comfort in a fragment of text from the Book he loved so well: " 'Because ye have been with me from the beginning.' Mr. Faber was my first customer, you know." Ethel had looked at the bottle, and then at Ralph, her eyes asking permission to accept, and Ralph had nodded very quickly. With a warm smile she had thanked August, and then deftly extracted the cork with her teeth.

They liked to recall how they had sat down then and there and drunk the quart, round after round, until it was all gone. It was not good gin, although three days old, but it was powerful. Gradually it loosened their tongues; they relaxed; they became friendlier. August, for the most part, limited his conversation to reiterated claims to perfect control over his thirst.

"I have the power to lay it down, and I have the power to take it again," he quoted from the Gospel according to St. John.

After the third drink the hostess dropped all affected restraint.

"Don't be formal," she said to August. "Call me Ethel. Can you pronounce it?"

"I can," he replied, "Ethel."

They congratulated him and took another drink.

"By the way," he added, rising politely, "my name is Ehler—August Ehler—Gus to my friends. Call me Gus."

Ralph extended his hand and the two men shook.

"I'm pleased to meet you, Mr. Ehler," Ralph said. "I'd been intending for some time to ask you your name."

"Gus," Ehler corrected him. "Don't call me Mister—call me Gus. Good ol' Gus Ehler—Honest Gus Ehler. I want you to call me Gus."

"Gus," said Ralph. Ethel said "Gussie!" Ehler laughed heartily and slapped her on the back.

"No hard feelings," he said. "Good ol' Gus Ehler—everybody's friend."

The next drink was the last in the quart. Gaily Ethel upturned the bottle over her own head to show that it was empty.

"Sempty," she explained.

"Salright," Gus replied, and went and got one of Ralph's quarts. They drank the second bottle. . . .

August's business was growing, even then at the start, by leaps and bounds, and soon the gifts to Ethel became mellower and more palatable. The gin gave way to authentic bonded stuff, rye, bourbon and Scotch, warm and cheery, softening the nerves and senses, casting a golden glow over all the world. Ethel presently dropped the formality of asking permission of Ralph before accepting each of the never-ending sequence of bottles. His nod had grown quicker and quicker. After a time he discontinued his semimonthly purchase of a case of gin and drank Ethel's presents.

Eventually, then, the rye and bourbon were displaced by fancier drinks, rare boozes which had been only names to Ethel. August brought thick black liqueurs from Spain; dynamic concoctions that came in on ships from Russia; mellow brandies and soothing sauternes from France. He brought anisette, sugary and almost imperceptibly sharp; champagne that rang in Ethel's head like wild silver bells on a frosty night; and pot-bellied little bottles of crème de menthe. He gave her rum from Jamaica, which she swigged down like water; Irish whiskey, which upset her stomach; schnapps, which burned her mouth so fiercely that she had to wash it down with a large tumblerful of Scotch. He brought real beer.

Once there was dry Curaçao for her. Another time August brought a Mexican favorite, mescal, which gave Ralph a slight touch of delirium tremens. On still another evening, for a lark, they drank gin, for the sake of auld lang syne. Never, though, was the Scotch replaced. Always, even when there were other bottles, Gus stood a sturdy brown bottle at Ethel's elbow, for better than anything else did she love Scotch.

Every evening they spent together, sitting around the large table in the Fabers' dining room, drinking and singing and crying. Ethel sang little snatches of love ballads, some of them very sad. Ralph joined in on everything. Gus sang hymns.

It was not long before Gus bought a car, a long, low, twelve-cylinder machine, with a purple body trimmed in narrow yellow stripes. Then they varied their evenings by driving out to drink their liquor in the fresh, sweet air of the open country. They were merry little outings, and generally, on the way home, they were in high spirits, as mettlesome and mischievous as school children on a holiday. Ralph and Gus threw empty bottles at farmhouse windows, and Ethel tied a cow's tail to the rear axle once and drove a mile or so down the road before the boys noticed it. They came home refreshed and hungry and still thirsty.

Always on these outings, Gus noticed, Ethel clung to the bottle of Scotch which he gave her each evening as her own special property. It aroused in him a feeling of tender indulgence, a warm fondness, to note her childish gratitude for it and the fierce determination with which she clutched the bottle by the neck, as a babe, he told himself, clutched its own little bottle of milk. It was the mother instinct in her. He and Ralph drank whatever else they had brought along, sharing only an infrequent round of their exotic beverages with her. Only rarely did they take a single drink from her Scotch.

Two or three times, early in their friendship, Ralph urged Gus to make the party a foursome by bringing along a woman friend. He suggested the names of several, and Gus, plainly embarrassed, rejected them all.

"All these are the beginning of sorrows," he quoted from the Gospel according to St. Matthew. But his eyes rested on Ethel, and she, whenever she could see him, dropped hers. Once she seconded Ralph's suggestion. At the look she saw in Gus's eyes she faltered, her voice broke and, to cover her confusion, she turned the bottle of Scotch up to her lips. When finally she lowered it, she saw the look still there. She never suggested another woman again. She was beginning to understand.

II

Beginning to understand? No, she already understood. She realized she did. More interesting was to become aware that she returned this love. She was, for the moment, panic-stricken. It savored of treachery to Ralph. Then she set herself to justifying it. She tried long and hard to convince herself that this new love was right, that Ralph's treatment of her had been such as to alienate her affections, that Gus was a better man, a worthier man, Ralph's superior in every way. And soon, naturally, she was successful.

Greatly relieved at scaling this sentimental barrier, she enjoyed herself with reckoning the score against Ralph. His actions since they had developed Gus as a friend and provider were calculated, consciously or unconsciously, to force her into the bootlegger's arms. That first slight, when he had interposed no objections to her accepting presents from him, other occasions when she had argued, as much with her own conscience as with Ralph, over this same question of propriety, and miscellaneous other incidents she was able to recall all brought Ralph into one aspect: he was exploiting her attractions to line his locker.

Briefly and bluntly, she was pleased to find Ralph had been offering Gus her company in return for his liquor. It was as plain as the nose on her face.

She thought of Gus with the greatest tenderness, now that she had disposed of the obstacles to loving him. He was as old as she, perhaps older, and could doubtless drink her under the table five nights out of the seven, and yet she thought of him as a boy, a charming, unspoiled youth. Associating with men of the world every day, doing business with them constantly, it seemed to her that he had been able to retain an amazingly great part of his childish sweetness. She found in his propensity for quoting from the Scripture a residue of an early religious training that had softened and made holy his only poorly concealed love for her. It was, she saw, different, far different, from this practical emotion she had found in Ralph. It was rarer, purer.

Gus never permitted a word of this love to pass his lips, though words could have told nothing his eyes had not already said a thousand times. Perhaps his conscience, a strict conscience, forbade this treachery to a friend, who in addition had been a very good customer. He certainly had all the opportunities he could have wanted, but he never spoke. He only looked, and Ethel understood.

And it was she who touched off this smoldering passion. It was on one of their drives into the country in quest of fresh air. Indirectly Ralph was responsible. Gus had brought three of the little pot-bellied bottles of crème de menthe, two bottles of cognac, a quart of absinthe, and the inevitable Scotch, for the evening's entertainment, and when he went out of the house to put the lap robes in the car, Ethel saw Ralph make a surreptitious snatch across the table. The quart of absinthe disappeared. Then he stole out of the room.

Quietly she followed him. He was in the library. As she entered she was just in time to see the last of the absinthe drain through the neck of the bottle into his open mouth. When Gus arrived in answer to her whoops he found Ralph having a convulsion.

Determined that the evening should not be spoiled, they lifted him out of the house and into the car. Gus directed the chauffeur to drive directly out of town. Neither the cold air nor the stimulants they gave him served to revive the stricken man. They made numerous lackadaisical efforts to open his eyes, and then, having failed altogether, they covered his recumbent form with a robe and sat back to enjoy the drive.

Ethel more than half expected some form or other of confession of love then and there. The opportunity was ideal; Ralph was as good as dead. She was positive Gus had not missed the answering light which had come into her eyes. She was certain that he knew his love was returned. But he remained silent. His soft, hurt eyes stared straight ahead. Methodically he lifted a bottle of cognac to his lips again and again, but he did not look around. His body was tense. His free hand gripped the edge of the seat. He seemed to be holding himself together only by a tremendous effort.

Slowly, almost unconsciously, she allowed her hand to slip toward his. There was an electric shock when she touched it that thrilled them both. Startled, she stopped; and then, encouraged by his failure to relieve his strained nerves by a shriek, she moved her hand again, and closed it over his. His knuckles, that were white with tension, flushed a rosy pink, which crept over his body until it appeared on his neck above his white collar. When, after slowly spreading over his entire surface, he felt that it had at last reached even his feet, he nearly swooned from the sweet excitement.

Then, before he could realize it, she was whispering to him, leaning against his shoulder, pressing her cheek against his. "Gus, Gus!" It was music, precious music to his ears. He closed his eyes, but he loosened his grip on the seat. Carefully, hampered though he was by her caress, he put the cork in the cognac bottle with his teeth, and laid it on the floor. Then he prepared himself to be ready when his self-control should break down.

He became conscious that she was pulling at his hand, the while she kept whispering his name. He relaxed, permitted her to do what she would with his hand, and then, when he felt her raising it, he stiffened again. His eyes being already shut, he had no need to shut them ecstatically. He waited. She carried his hand to her lips, and they pressed warm and damp and sticky against each finger. Then she lowered it to her bosom. He caught the little gasp she gave. Then, suddenly, impulsively, she pressed it tight, tight, tight against the bottle of Scotch. With a partly stifled cry he caught her to him. His reserve swept away, all caution abandoned, nothing there but the wild love of a man for a woman, he rained kisses, hot, fierce, passionate kisses, rained them furiously, savagely, on her cheeks, her eyes, her mouth, her chin, her neck, the bottle of Scotch. . . .

III

Before he left her that evening he whispered a promise to return the next morning. She stood before him, a faraway look in her eyes, a pitiful little trickle of whiskey dried on her chin. She did not understand. Gently he took the empty bottle from her unresisting hand and stood it on the chauffeur's head, and repeated the promise. She melted into his arms and, as Ralph was having another convulsion and paying no heed to anything else, they kissed goodnight.

She received him the next morning in the dining room. A smile, half sadness, half pleasure, was on her face as he entered. The room, when she glanced about it, appeared a strange place, one she had not seen ever, or for a long time. But over it hung the fragrance of old, sweet pleasures. Her glance rested on a dent in the floor, where at the end of one of their evenings Ralph had started to gnaw his way to Australia. There was a bent bracket on the chandelier, where she had looped the loop on another occasion. And on the ceiling was a large green spot, where Gus had splashed several dollars' worth of spinach once, saying, "I will not any more eat thereof," attributing it to the Gospel according to St. Luke. But the memories brought sadness, for the night had been spent in thought and prayer, and the conclusion she had reached was not an easy one to carry out.

It was another Gus that appeared before her. The boyish solemnity was gone from his face. In its place was strength, a look of sternness born of determination; there was a glint of exaltation in his eye. She thought suddenly of his true resemblance to one of the apostles. Her head ached.

She met his embrace, clinging to him, her heart overflowing with emotion. Madly he caressed her, and whispered in her ear: "Dear heart, how are you?" She returned the whisper: "Fairly well. How are you?" "Great," he whispered in reply. They unclasped and sat down.

Quickly he cleared the ground for his subject. Where was Ralph? Had she taken her Bromo Seltzer? Did she remember all? Without waiting for replies he hurried on:

"Ethel, we've got to get out of here. This waiting, this suspense, must end. You must go to Montreal; I'll go to New Orleans. You must get a divorce—at once. There will be no

talk, no gossip, nothing against your character. I'll protect
you in every way. But we—"

"Gus, Gus!" Her voice was low and throbbing with anguish. "If only it were possible!"

"But it is, dearest, it is. Another week, a month—"

"No, no, you don't understand. It isn't time, it isn't fear,
that prevents it, dear Gus. It is something deeper, something bigger. It is my church."

"I—I don't understand, Ethel."

His faltering voice tore into her heart like a knife, but she
steeled herself to do what she had decided was right.

"You forget, dear," she said gently, "that my church does
not sanction divorce and remarriage. In the eyes of my
church that is sin. And, Gus, would you have me if—"

His eyes blazed as he sprang to his feet.

"Your church!" he shot at her. "Would a good church
stand between a woman and the man she loves?"

"August!" She stiffened, her eyes flashed, and instantly
he was contrite.

"But Ethel—dearest—don't you see—"

She softened and touched a kiss to his temple.

"I see, dear Gussie, but what else is there to do? I will not,
I cannot, go counter to my church. It would not be right."

He must have sensed the note of strength in her voice, for
he got to his feet, his face red with conflicting emotions. He
reached the buffet in a bound and poured himself a stiff
drink. It seemed to calm him. He spoke more rationally.

"I cannot understand a church," he said, "that could be
so terrible. I cannot understand one that insists on your
staying married to a man who is not your equal in any way,
a man whom you no longer love. It cannot be!"

"I should have told you last night," she murmured. "I am
not free to love, no matter what sort of a man I have married. And I can never be free until he is dead—or I."

"Dead!"

"Yes, dead. Not until he is dead. There is no alternative.
While he lives I am his. Only death can help me. And he is
in such good health."

Gus stood as if transfixed.

"Dead!" he murmured. The word burned into his mind. "Ashes to ashes, dust to dust," he quoted. And then when he spoke to her again there was a new light, a light of hope in his eyes.

"Dearest," he said, "I have faith. 'The just shall live by faith.' Our love must not die."

"Only death," Ethel repeated softly, "only death can free me."

The bootlegger poured himself another drink. He started back to her side once, and then, on second thought, returned to the buffet and the bottle. His somber eyes studied her through the dark amber of the liquor. She rose and joined him.

"Here's laughing at you," she toasted him, a forced gaiety in her voice.

His eyes held dark and heavy.

"Death," he repeated, but he drank with her.

They stood looking at each other, a strained silence between them. They took another drink. Ethel put her arms around his neck.

"Gus," she said tenderly, "we must be careful. We must take care of ourselves against doing wrong. Perhaps— some day—who can tell—we may belong to each other. But not now, dear. We must cast the thought aside. I have done wrong, I have been a faithless wife, to say these things to you, but I couldn't help it, Gus. I wanted you to know."

He did not speak at once. His thoughts were far away, and bitter. He was thinking of himself. Wealthy, talented, possessed of professional and social position, master of more money than he would ever need for himself alone, he was powerless before this woman's sturdy adherence to her faith. It stirred him. "One of God's good women," he murmured. Other women could be had, dozens of them, moths ready to flutter to his flame, but—this was the woman he wanted. And finding her, he was helpless. A Methodist himself, he could not understand this objection to divorce.

"Ethel," he said, "you are a good woman, 'the noblest work of God.' Forgive me, dear, if I have offended you."

Her reply was to raise her lips to his. He set the glass down on the buffet and embraced her.

"Continue in prayer," he whispered to her, "and watch in the same with thanksgiving."

An hour later, when Ralph came downstairs, he found Ethel alone, sitting in the window seat, staring out over the city. Gus had gone. Without turning, she pointed toward the buffet. Without speaking, Ralph poured himself a drink. Without falling, he climbed on top of the buffet and went to sleep.

IV

Gus's thoughts, when he returned to his offices, were in a state of chaos. He spoke sharply to the office boy in the vestibule. He snapped at the stenographers in the outer office. He was cross to the clerks in the accounting office. He glared at the people waiting for him in the anteroom. He was abrupt to his secretary.

"Get rid of them," he said curtly. "Tell them anything."

For an hour he sat struggling with his emotions. He thought of Ethel, and pity welled in his heart at the idea of her bound to a man she did not love. And yet against Ralph he felt no direct hatred. True, he realized, he was unworthy of her. He had mistreated her. He had robbed her—he had not failed to notice the discontinuance of the semimonthly purchase of a case of gin or of the avidity with which Ralph seized the bottles he had brought to Ethel. He had ignored these things for her sake. But he had noticed them, and others too: Ralph's habitual failure to pour the first drink for his wife, his frugality when he did pour for her, the envy in his eyes at the sight of her bottle of Scotch.

"The face of the Lord is against them that do evil," he reflected. "And the end of all these things is at hand; be ye sober."

His reverie was at length interrupted by a hesitating knock at the door. The secretary brought word of the presence outside of Antonio Madoni, of the importing firm of Madoni & Feronella.

"Show him in," Gus ordered, shaking his thoughts from him.

Madoni entered, a little Italian with a perpetual smile and a roving, wary eye.

Gus greeted him without enthusiasm. "More excuses, I suppose," he said. "This is the last time. Go on and tell me, the shipment is still delayed. You want me to give you more time. Right?"

Madoni smiled on.

"Ah, Mist' Ehla," he said, "she's a beet late. Whatta you care? You gotta plent' booze. She be in soon-a now. You wanta some gin?"

Gus regarded the Italian coldly.

"I don't sell gin any more, and you know it."

Unabashed the Italian smilingly enumerated the qualities of this new lot.

"Only a leetla beet. You tak-a dees gin. She's al-a-right dees gin she is. She got-a da Gordon labels on."

"Where'd you get it?" Gus asked.

From a friend, a druggist, likewise an Italian. No, he didn't know when it was made. But it had Gordon labels on. Madoni had the highest faith in the manufacturer.

"I gotta da case downstairs," he wheedled. "Mebbe I let you have it for not'in'. Try it. Fine-a stuff I got."

Gus thought it over. "Bring it up," he told him finally, and presently one of Madoni's subordinates lifted it into the office and laid it on the desk. Gus drew the cork from a bottle with his teeth. He poured two glasses.

"Let's see how it goes," he said.

Madoni smilingly pushed the proffered glass back.

"Nev-a touch-a da stuff," he said. "None-a da booze for mine."

Gus smelled his glass. Then he studied the Italian intently. He smelled the drink again, and then the bottle. Finally he poured the two drinks back into the bottle and corked it. He pressed a button and the secretary came in.

"Call a taxi," he said.

Madoni and his subordinates moved to the door. Gus put on his coat and followed them. They shook hands, and the Italians left. When the taxi came Gus sent the secretary down with the case of gin. He followed it shortly. A minute later he and the case of gin were speeding toward Rose Crest Heights.

Ethel did not attempt to conceal her surprise at his early return, and at the sight of the case being brought in she clapped her hands with pleasure; she thought it was Scotch. Gus patted her shoulder. "It's gin," he said tenderly. She pouted charmingly, until he produced a pint flask from each hip pocket. "Scotch," he said. With a little cry of pleasure she pressed them to her heart.

He led her into the dining room. Ralph still lay asleep on the buffet. Gus glanced at him once, but said nothing. Ethel brought out two glasses and they drained the two pints before speaking.

"Not my will, O Lord, but Thine be done," he murmured.

"Gus—" she began.

"Hush," he commanded, and suddenly she realized there was something ominous about his air, something threatening, menacing. She did not understand it, and it frightened her strangely. He drew her to the divan and they sat down together. She tried to speak again, and again he warned her. She tried to catch his hand; it was clenched and hard. She looked up into his face fearfully and saw that his eyes were fixed on Ralph's still form. He was staring steadily, relentlessly. Involuntarily her eyes followed his.

Then, through the long afternoon, they watched together, neither moving nor speaking. Their eyes did not leave the inert figure. The ray of sun through the west window lengthened and flattened. At long, dreary intervals a clock struck somewhere—three, four, five o'clock. The room grew dark, and night came. Still they did not move, nor did Ralph.

At five-thirty Ethel, her nerves stretched to the breaking-point, shaking and throbbing and weak in every member, rose and with a little half-hysterical cry rushed across the room to the buffet. Gus rose to restrain her, but she motioned him back. She picked up the heavy, silver-inlaid corkscrew and gouged Ralph's knuckles with its point. His hand relaxed and she snatched the half-empty bottle of Scotch from it. With a little moan of pleasure she raised it to her lips, and did not lower it until it was empty. Then, refreshed, she returned to Gus's side.

They took up the vigil again, now in the semidark, but it was not long they had to wait. The gouge in the knuckles had aroused Ralph. He stirred once or twice convulsively, shifting his position.

At length, after several unsuccessful efforts, he lifted his head. With bleared, nearly closed eyes he glanced about the room, seeing nothing. Gus and Ethel, still as death, watched him from a darkened angle of the room. Ralph studied the situation for some time, though betraying no particular interest in it. Then he raised himself to his elbow, to his knees, swaying perilously, and finally he gained his feet. He stood straight up on top of the buffet, mumbling to himself. The watchers saw him grope in the air for a moment, and then try to step down the four feet to the floor. He fell, striking head first, and scrambled to his feet, giggling.

"I'm down," they heard him say.

He made his way to the center table, propped himself against it, and from there studied the room again. His roving eyes came to rest on the case of gin. Electrified he reached for it and ripped off the top. Gus drew Ethel closer to him. Their hands clasped. They waited tensely for they knew not what. They could hear Ralph chortling as he discovered the contents of the case. And he mumbled incoherently as he extracted the cork from a bottle.

Then the mumblings were hushed. In their place came gurgles, long and deep. Finally a hollow one, as he pulled his mouth away. They saw him, silhouetted against the window, set the bottle again on the table. Then he collapsed into a chair. For a moment he seemed comfortable; then his legs began to stiffen. The chair screeched as his writhing body strained in it. His head fell back. His whole body stiffened. There was a blood-chilling rattle in his throat. Then he lay still.

A minute of silence passed. The room was like death. Ethel was half-unconscious from the tension, the horror of the unknown. She could only clutch Gus's hand. Then he shook himself loose from her. He rose unsteadily and went over to the chair. He produced a small mirror from his pocket and held it before Ralph's open mouth. He took it to the window and looked at it, after which he went out into the hall.

She heard him take the receiver from the phone. He called a number.

"Is this Madoni? . . . This is Ehler speaking. I've called to let you know I don't think I'll take that consignment after all. . . . Yes, I mean the gin. . . . No, it's not the price; I've just got a hunch it's not all right. . . . Yes, I'll pay for this case. I'll send a check in the morning. Good-by."

"Ethel," he said, coming back into the room and pulling her into his arms, "the Lord giveth and the Lord taketh away." He kissed her gently on the top of the head. "And His ways are inscrutable. We, poor sinners, can only accept His mandates as we in our poor way can interpret them. If He saw fit . . . ashes to ashes, dust to dust. It is His will, and of sinners did He say 'And these shall go into everlasting punishment' "—he pressed her closer—" 'but the righteous into life everlasting.' Are you happy now, dearest?"

She snuggled in his arms with a little purr of contentment.

A Letter

§ BY ISAAC BABEL

Translated by Babette Deutsch

THIS is a letter home dictated to me by Kurdyukov, a boy
who runs errands for us here at headquarters. It deserves
to be saved from oblivion. I have copied it out with no
embellishments, and I give it here word for word, in all
honesty.

"Dear Mama, Yevdokiya Fyodorovna. In the first place I
hasten to inform you that, the Lord be praised, I am alive
and well, which I would like to hear the same from you.
And also I bow very low before you—my white brow to the
damp earth." (Here follows an enumeration of relatives,
godparents, cronies. Let's omit that. Let's go on to the next
paragraph.)

"Dear Mama, Yevdokiya Fyodorovna Kurdyukova. I hasten to write you that I am with Comrade Budyonny's Red
Cavalry, and so is your crony, Nikon Vasilich, who you
should know is now a Red Hero. Nikon Vasilich made a
place for me with him in the office of the Political Section
where we supply the front with literature and papers: the
Moscow *Izvestia* of the Central Executive Committee, the

Moscow *Pravda,* and our own merciless paper, *The Red Trooper,* that every fighter at the front wants to get hold of and after he has read it he whacks at the dirty Polish gentry with heroic spirit and I being with Nikon Vasilich live like a lord.

"Dear Mama, Yevdokiya Fyodorovna. Send me whatever you possibly can. I beg you to slaughter the spotted pig and make up a package for me addressed to Vasily Kurdyukov, in care of Comrade Budyonny's Political Section. Every day I lie down to rest with nothing in my stomach and without any clothes so that I am mighty cold. Write me a letter about my Styopa, is he alive or not, I beg you to look after him and write me about him—does he still knock one leg against the other as he walks or has he stopped that, and also about the scab on his forelegs, has he been shod or hasn't he? I beg you, dear Mama, Yevdokiya Fyodorovna, do wash his forelegs without fail with the soap that I left behind the icons and if Dad did away with the soap be sure to buy some at Krasnodar and God will not forsake you. I can also tell you that the country hereabouts isn't good for much, the peasants take their horses and hide themselves in the woods from our Red eagles, you don't see much wheat, and what you see is no account, it makes us laugh. People sow rye and oats too. Hops grow here on sticks, which makes it very neat; they make home-brew of it.

"In the second place I hasten to tell you about Dad, that he did in my brother Fyodor Timofeyich Kurdyukov, a good year ago. Our Red Brigade under Comrade Pavlichenko was marching on the city of Rostov at that time and treason broke out in our ranks and Dad was company commander then with the Whites under Denikin. Them as saw him said he wore medals on him like under the old regime. And on account of that treason going on we were all captured by the Whites, and Dad's eye lit on brother Fyodor Timofeyich. And Dad began to pitch into brother Fyodor Timofeyich saying, 'You scum! You Red dog! You son of a bitch!' and such things and he kept it up till dark when it was all up with brother Fyodor Timofeyich. At the time I wrote you a letter about how your Fedya lies without a cross over him. But Dad caught me with the letter and said: 'You boys, you're your mother's children, you're of her stock, the huzzy, I used to give your mother a big belly and I'll do it again, my life is done for, for the sake of justice I'll stamp out my own seed,' and he went on that way. I suffered at his hands like our Savior Jesus Christ. But pretty soon I ran away from Dad and managed to join my unit again under Comrade Pavlichenko. And our brigade got orders to move on to the city of Voronezh to get reinforcements and there we got reinforcements and horses too, knapsacks, guns, and all the rest of it. About Voronezh I can tell you, dear Mama, Yevdokiya Fyodorovna, that that's a very splendid town, lots bigger than Krasnodar, the people there are very good-looking and you can go bathing in the river. They gave us two pounds of bread a day, half a pound of meat, and sugar according, so when we got up of a morning we had sweetened tea to drink, likewise in the evening, and we forgot that there ever was a famine, and at dinnertime I used to go to brother Semyon Timofeyich where they had pancakes and roast goose, and after that I used to lie down to rest. The whole regiment those days wanted to have brother Semyon Timofeyich as commander on account of his being such a desperate fellow and Comrade Budyonny issued an order that it should be so and he got two horses, an outfit in fine condition, a cart all for his own stuff and the Order of the Red Flag, and here was me reckoned as his brother. So now if any neighbor starts to get fresh with you, Semyon Timofeyich is fully in a position to skin him alive. And then we started to chase General Denikin and we slaughtered thousands of them and drove them into the Black Sea, but Dad was nowhere to be seen and Semyon Timofeyich was looking for him all along the front because he missed brother Fedya so badly. Only, dear Mama, you know Dad and his pigheaded ways, so here's what he goes and does—he has the impudence to dye his red beard black and he stays in the city of Maikop dressed up like a civilian so that none of the citizens there could tell that here was the same man as was constable under the old regime. Only, mark you, truth will out, Nikon Vasilich, your crony, happened to see him in somebody's house and wrote a letter to Semyon Timofeyich. We jumped into the saddle and rode two hundred versts—I, brother Senka, and some other Cossack boys from our village back home who wanted to come along.

"And what did we see in the city of Maikop? We saw that the rear is always at odds with the front and is lousy with treason and with Jews like under the old regime. And at Maikop Semyon Timofeyich made it hot for the dirty Jews because they wouldn't give Dad up but they put him in jail under lock and key and they said they had orders from Comrade Trotzky not to kill prisoners, 'we will try him ourselves,' they said, 'don't worry, he'll get what's coming to him.' But Semyon Timofeyich insisted on his rights and he showed them that he was the commander of a regiment and that Comrade Budyonny had given him all the Orders of the Red Flag and he threatened to kill everybody who rowed with him over Dad's person and refused to hand him over and the boys from back home made the same threat. In the end Semyon Timofeyich got Dad all right and began to horsewhip him and he lined up all the fighting men in the yard in proper military order. And then Senka splashed some water on Dad's beard and the dye ran off it and Senka asked Dad Timofey Rodionovich:

" 'You're in my hands now, Dad, do you feel good?'

" 'No,' says Dad, 'I don't feel good.'

"Then Senka asked: 'And Fedya, when you were doing him in, did he feel good?'

" 'No,' says Dad, 'he didn't.'

"Then Senka asked: 'And did you think, Dad, that one day it would go bad with you?'

" 'No,' says Dad, 'I didn't think that it would go bad with me.'

"Then Senka turned to the men and said: 'And I guess, Dad, if I once get into your hands you won't spare me either. And now, Dad, we'll make an end of you.'

"And Timofey Rodionovich started to curse Senka shamelessly, using his mother's name and that of the Holy Virgin, and he punched his jaw for him plenty, and Semyon Timofeyich sent me out of the yard so that, dear Mama, Yevdokiya Fyodorovna, I cannot describe to you how they did Dad in because I was sent out of the yard.

"After that we were stationed in the city of Novorossisk. As regards this town I can tell you that beyond it there isn't any more land but only water, the Black Sea, and we stayed there right on till May when we pulled up stakes and moved on to the Polish front and ever since then we've been at work trouncing the Polish gentry . . .

"I remain your dear son, Vasily Timofeyich Kurdyukov. Mom, do look after Styopa and God will not forsake you . . ."

That is Kurdyukov's letter, not a word of which has been changed. When I finished it he took the written sheet and tucked it into his bosom against the bare skin.

"Kurdyukov," I said to the boy, "was your father a bad lot?"

"My father was a dog," he answered grimly.

"And what about your mother?"

"My mother—she's all right. If you please, here is the whole family. . . ."

He handed me a broken photograph. It showed Timofey Kurdyukov, stiff, broad-shouldered, wearing his policeman's càp, his beard carefully combed, with knobby cheekbones, a bright stare in his vacant colorless eyes. Beside him, seated in a bamboo armchair, shimmered a tiny peasant woman in a bloused waist, with a clear, shy, withered face. And against the photographer's screen, a miserable provincial affair with flowers and doves, towered two boys, enormous hulking fellows, stolid, broadfaced, goggle-eyed, as rigid as if at drill—the two Kurdyukov brothers, Fyodor and Semyon.

Winter

BY KIT REED

It was late fall when he come to us, there was a scum of ice on all the puddles and I could feel the winter cold and fearsome in my bones, the hunger inside me was already uncurling, it would pace through the first of the year but by spring it would be raging like a tiger, consuming me until the thaw when Maude could hunt again and we would get the truck down the road to town. I was done canning but I got the tomatoes we had hanging in the cellar and I canned some more; Maude went out and brought back every piece of meat she could shoot and all the grain and flour and powdered milk she could bring in one truckload, we had to lay in everything we could before the snow could come and seal us in. The week he come Maude found a jack rabbit stone dead in the road, it was frozen with its feet sticking straight up, and all the meat hanging in the cold room had frozen. Friday there was rime on the grass and when I looked out I seen footprints in the rime, I said Maude, someone is in the playhouse and we went out and there he was. He was asleep in the mess of clothes we always dressed up in, he had his head on the velvet gown my mother wore to the Exposition and his feet

197

on the satin gown she married Father in, he had pulled her feather boa around his neck and her fox fur was wrapped around his loins.

Before he come, Maude and me would pass the winter talking about how it used to be, we would call up the past between us and look at it and Maude would end by blaming me. I could of married either Lister Hoffman or Harry Mead and left this place for good if it hadn't been for you, Lizzie. I'd tell her, Hell, I never needed you. You didn't marry them because you didn't marry them, you was scared of it and you would use me for an excuse. She would get mad then. It's a lie. Have it your way, I would tell her, just to keep the peace.

We both knew I would of married the first man that asked me, but nobody would, not even with all my money, nobody would ask me because of the taint. If nobody had of known then some man might of married me, but I went down to the field with Miles Harrison once while Father was still alive, and Miles and me, we almost, except that the blackness took me, right there in front of him, and so I never did. Nobody needed to know, but then Miles saw me fall down in the field. I guess it was him that put something between my teeth, but when I come to myself he was gone. Next time I went to town they all looked at me funny, some of them would try and face up to me and be polite but they was all jumpy, thinking would I do it right there in front of them, would I froth much, would they be hurt, as soon as was decent they would say Excuse me, I got to, anything to get out of there fast. When I run into Miles that day he wouldn't look at me and there hasn't been a man near me since then, not in more than fifty years, but Miles and me, we almost, and I have never stopped thinking about that.

Now Father is gone and my mother is gone and even Lister Hoffman and Miles Harrison and half the town kids that used to laugh at me, they are all gone, but Maude still reproaches me, we sit after supper and she says If it hadn't been for you I would have grandchildren now and I tell her

I would have had them before ever she did because she never liked men, she would only suffer them to get children and that would be too much trouble, it would hurt. That's a lie, Lizzie, she would say, Harry and me used to . . . and I would tell her You never, but Miles and me . . . Then we would both think about being young and having people's hands on us but memory turns Maude bitter and she can never leave it at that, she says, It's all your fault, but I know in my heart that people make their lives what they want them, and all she ever wanted was to be locked in here with nobody to make demands on her, she wanted to stay in this house with me, her dried-up sister, cold and safe, and if the hunger is on her, it has come on her late.

After a while we would start to make up stuff: Once I went with a boy all the way to Portland . . . Once I danced all night and half the morning, he wanted to kiss me on the place where my elbow bends . . . We would try to spin out the winter but even that was not enough and so we would always be left with the hunger; no matter how much we laid in, the meat was always gone before the thaw and I suppose it was really our lives we was judging but we would decide nothing in the cans looked good to us and so we would sit and dream and hunger and wonder if we would die of it, but finally the thaw would come and Maude would look at me and sigh: If only we had another chance.

Well now perhaps we will.

We found him in the playhouse, maybe it was seeing him asleep in the middle of my mother's clothes or maybe it was being in the playhouse, where we pretended so many times, but there was this boy, or man, and something about him called up our best memories, there was promise wrote all over him. I am too old, I am all dried out, but I have never stopped thinking about that one time and seeing that boy there, I could pretend he was Miles and I was still young. I guess he sensed us, he woke up fast and went into a crouch, maybe he had a knife, and then I guess he saw it was just two big old ladies in Army boots, he said,

I run away from the Marines, I needed a place to sleep.

Maude said, I don't care what you need, you got to get out of here, but when he stood up he wobbled. His hair fell across his head like the hair on a boy I used to know and I said, Maude, why don't you say yes to something just this once.

He had on this denim shirt and pants like no uniform I ever seen and he was saying, Two things happened, I found out I might have to shoot somebody in the war and then I made a mistake and they beat me so I cut out of there. He smiled and he looked open. I stared hard at Maude and Maude finally looked at me and said, All right, come up to the house and get something to eat.

He said his name was Arnold but when we asked him Arnold what, he said Never mind. He was in the kitchen by then, he had his head bent over a bowl of oatmeal and some biscuits I had made, and when I looked at Maude she was watching the way the light slid across his hair. When we told him our names he said, You are both beautiful ladies, I could see Maude's hands go up to her face and she went into her room and when she come back I saw she had put color on her cheeks. While we was alone he said how good the biscuits was and wasn't that beautiful silver, did I keep it polished all myself and I said well yes, Maude brings in supplies but I am in charge of the house and making all the food. She come back then and saw us with our heads together and said to Arnold, I guess you'll be leaving soon.

I don't know, he said, they'll be out looking for me with guns and dogs.

That's no never mind of ours.

I never done nothing bad in the Marines, we just had different ideas. We both figured it was something worse but he looked so sad and tired and besides, it was nice to have him to talk to, he said, I just need a place to hole up for a while.

Maude said, You could always go back to your family.

He said, They never wanted me. They was always mean-hearted, not like you.

I took her aside and said, It wouldn't kill you to let him stay on, Maude, it's time we had a little life around here.

There won't be enough food for three.

He won't stay long. Besides, he can help you with the chores.

She was looking at his bright hair again, she said, like it was all my doing, If you want to let him stay I guess we can let him stay.

He was saying, I could work for my keep.

All right, I said, you can stay on until you get your strength.

My heart jumped. A man, I thought. A man. How can I explain it? It was like being young, having him around. I looked at Maude and saw some of the same things in her eyes, hunger and hope, and I thought, You are ours now, Arnold, you are all ours. We will feed you and take care of you and when you want to wander we will let you wander, but we will never let you go.

Just until things die down a little, he was saying.

Maude had a funny grin. Just until things die down.

Well it must of started snowing right after dark that afternoon, because when we all waked up the house was surrounded, I said, Good thing you got the meat in, Maude, and she looked out, it was still blowing snow and it showed no signs of stopping, she looked out and said, I guess it is.

He was still asleep, he slept the day through except he stumbled down at dusk and dreamed over a bowl of my rabbit stew, I turned to the sink and when I looked back the stew was gone and the biscuits was gone and all the extra in the pot was gone, I had a little flash of fright, it was all disappearing too fast. Then Maude come over to me and hissed. The food, he's eating all the food and I looked at his brown hands and his tender neck and I said, It don't matter, Maude, he's young and strong and if we run short he can go out into the snow and hunt. When we looked around next time he was gone, he had dreamed his way through half a pie and gone right back to bed.

Next morning he was up before the light, we sat together

around the kitchen table and I thought how nice it was to
have a man in the house, I could look at him and imagine
anything I wanted. Then he got up and said, Look, I want to
thank you for everything, I got to get along now and I said,
You can't, and he said, I got things to do, I been here long
enough, but I told him You can't, and took him over to the
window. The sun was up by then and there it was, snow
almost to the window ledges, like we have every winter,
and all the trees was shrouded, we could watch the sun
take the snow and make it sparkle and I said, Beautiful
snow, beautiful, and he only shrugged and said, I guess I'll
have to wait till it clears off some. I touched his shoulder.
I guess it will. I knew not to tell him it would never clear off,
not until late spring; maybe he guessed, anyway he looked
so sad I gave him Father's silver snuffbox to cheer him up.

He would divide his time between Maude and me, he
played Rook with her and made her laugh so hard she gave
him her pearl earrings and the brooch Father brought her
back from Quebec. I gave him Grandfather's diamond
stickpin because he admired it, and for Christmas we gave
him the cameos and Father's gold-headed cane. Maude got
the flu over New Year and Arnold and me spent New Year's
Eve together, I mulled some wine and he hung up up some
of Mama's jewelery from the center light, and touched it
and made it twirl. We lit the candles and played the radio,
New Year's Eve in Times Square and somebody's Make-
believe Ballroom, I went to pour another cup of wine and
his hand was on mine on the bottle, I knew my lips was red
for once and next day I gave him Papa's fur-lined coat.

I guess Maude suspected there was something between
us, she looked pinched and mean when I went in with her
broth at lunch, she said, Where were you at breakfast and
I said, Maude it's New Year's Day, I thought I would like to
sleep in for once. She was quick and spiteful. You were
with him. I thought, If she wants to think that about me, let
her, and I let my eyes go sleepy and I said, We had to see the
New Year in, didn't we? She was out of bed in two days, I

have never seen anybody get up so fast after the flu. I think she couldn't stand us being where she couldn't see what we was up to every living minute. Then I got sick and I knew what torture it must have been for her, just laying there, I would call Maude and I would call her, and sometimes she would come and sometimes she wouldn't come and when she finally did look in on me I would say, Maude, where have you been and she would only giggle and not answer. There was meat cooking all the time, roasts and chops and chicken fricassee, when I said Maude, you're going to use it up, she would only smile and say, I just had to show him who's who in the kitchen, he tells me I'm a better cook than you ever was. After a while I got up, I had to even if I was dizzy and like to throw up, I had to get downstairs where I could keep an eye on them. As soon as I was up to it I made a roast of venison that would put hair on an egg and after that we would vie with each other in the kitchen, Maude and me. Once I had my hand on the skillet handle and she come over and tried to take it away, she was saying, Let me serve it up for him. I said, You're a fool, Maude, I cooked this and she hissed at me, through the steam, It won't do you no good, Lizzie, it's me he loves, and I just pushed her away and said, You goddam fool, he loves me, and I give him my amethysts just to prove it. A couple of days later I couldn't find neither of them nowhere, I thought I heard noises up in the back room and I went up there and if they was in there they wouldn't answer, the door was locked and they wouldn't say nothing, not even when I knocked and knocked and knocked. So the next day I took him up in my room and we locked the door and I told him a story about every piece in my jewel box, even the cheap ones, when Maude tapped and whined outside the door we would just shush, and when we did come out and she said, All right, Lizzie, what was you doing in there, I only giggled and wouldn't tell.

She shouldn't of done it, we was all sitting around the table after dinner and she looked at me hard and said, You know something, Arnold, I wouldn't get too close to Lizzie, she has fits. Arnold only tried to look like it didn't matter, but after Maude went to bed I went down to make sure it was all right. He was still in the kitchen, whittling, and when I tried to touch his hand he pulled away.

I said, Don't be scared, I only throw one in a blue moon.

He said, That don't matter.

Then what's the matter?

I don't know, Miss Lizzie, I just don't think you trust me.

Course I trust you, Arnold, don't I give you everything?

He just looked sad. Everything but trust.

I owe you so much, Arnold, you make me feel so young.

He just smiled for me then. You look younger, Miss Lizzie, you been getting younger every day I been here.

You did it.

If you let me, I could make you really young.

Yes, Arnold, yes.

But I have to know you trust me.

Yes, Arnold.

So I showed him where the money was. By then it was past midnight and we was both tired, he said, Tomorrow, and I let him go off to his rest.

I don't know what roused us both and brought us out into the hall but I bumped into Maude at dawn, we was both standing in our nightgowns like two ghosts. We crept downstairs together and there was light in the kitchen, the place where we kept the money was open, empty, and there was a crack of light in the door to the coldroom. I remember looking through and thinking, The meat is almost gone. Then we opened the door a crack wider and there he was, he had made a sledge, he must of sneaked down there and worked on it every night. It was piled with stuff, our stuff, and now he had the door to the outside open, he had dug himself a ramp out of the snow and he was lashing some homemade snowshoes on his feet, in another minute he would cut out of there.

When he heard us he turned.

I had the shotgun and Maude had the axe.

He said, You can have all your stuff.

We said, We don't care about the stuff, Arnold. How could we tell him it was our youth he was taking away?

He looked at us, wall-eyed. You can have it all, just let me out.

You said you loved us, Arnold.

He was scrabbling up the snow ramp. Never mind what I told you, let me out of here.

He was going to get away in another minute, so Maude let him have it with the axe.

Afterwards we closed the way to the outside and stood there and looked at each other, I couldn't say what was in my heart so I only looked at Maude, we was both sad, sad, I said, The food is almost gone.

Maude said, Everything is gone. We'll never make it to spring.

I said, We have to make it to spring.

Maude looked at him laying there. You know what he told me? He said, I can make you young.

Me too, I said. There was something in his eyes that made me believe it.

Maude's eyes was aglitter, she said, The food is almost gone.

I knew what she meant, he was going to make us young. I don't know how it will work in us, but he is going to make us young, it will be as if the fits had never took me, never in all them years. Maude was looking at me, waiting, and after a minute I looked square at her and said, I know.

So we et him.